FELICIA ST.
ABOUT

As much as I tried to ~~~~~~~~~~~~~~~
when news reached me that my brother was
missing, nothing could keep me away from Texas
in an effort to find him. Not even Dane Rineholt.

I've known Dane since I was a gangly adolescent.
Despite the years since then, he still treats me like a
teenager with a crush. Well, I've gotten over my
childhood fantasies about our ranch foreman. Now,
all I care about is finding Adam. I will tolerate
Dane's presence only because he's necessary to
the search.

Once Adam is found, though, I'm returning to my
other life—my life away from the ranch, from Texas
and from the man I've worked hard to forget.

Please address questions and book requests to: Silhouette Reader Service
U.S.: 3010 Walden Ave., P.O. Box 1325, Buffalo, NY 14269
Canadian: P.O. Box 609, Fort Erie, Ont. L2A 5X3

Reunited Hearts

WESTERN *Lovers*™

ANNETTE BROADRICK

RETURN TO YESTERDAY

Silhouette Books

Published by Silhouette Books

America's Publisher of Contemporary Romance

To the friendly people of Mason, Texas,
who made my stay there
both warm and welcome.

SILHOUETTE BOOKS
300 East 42nd St.,
New York, N.Y. 10017

ISBN 0-373-88536-9

RETURN TO YESTERDAY

Copyright © 1987 by Annette Broadrick

Printed in U.S.A.

One

Felicia St. Clair stared out the small, round window of the plane, watching the dark, swirling clouds surround the wingtip. As the plane descended from its long flight from Los Angeles to Austin, the local weather made itself felt. Driving rain beat against the fragile shell of the plane.

Ordinarily Felicia would have been nervous about the flight and the worsening weather, but ever since the phone call she'd received the night before, she had swung between an unnatural calm—while she made reservations to fly home, packed her clothes, called her boss to request an emergency leave of absence—and a sense of panic, which overcame her every time she thought about the message she had received.

Once again she forced herself into a semblance of calmness and tried to concentrate on the weather conditions. She hated flying, even in the finest weather. Therefore, under normal circumstances their present rough descent should have had her running screaming down the aisles. However, at the moment she scarcely noticed the turbulent gusts that had the stewardess apologizing to the passengers as she cautioned them to stay in their seats.

Felicia glanced down at her hands, gripped tightly together in her lap. She felt strange returning home to Texas after all of this time. Whenever she had tried to imagine a possible homecoming, she had always visualized her brother, Adam, there to greet her.

No matter how much she tried to direct her thoughts, they continued to return to Adam, with his contagious grin and sparkling eyes. Five years her senior, Adam had been the hub around which her life had revolved as a young girl. He'd taken the place of the father she'd never known, and after their mother had died, when Felicia was twelve, Adam had become parents and brother all rolled into one.

Thinking about Adam made the hollow feeling deep in the pit of her stomach more pronounced, the same feeling she'd had since Dane had called to tell her that Adam had disappeared somewhere in Mexico.

Please, God, don't let anything happen to Adam. She silently recited the same prayer she'd been repeating since Dane had called.

Adam was missing.

How could that be? Adam had always been there for her. He had picked her up, dusted her off, dried her tears—how many times? Over how many years?

Adam had always been there when she'd needed him. And never had Felicia needed him more than now, when in a few short hours she would be forced to see Dane Rineholt again and pretend he was no more to her than a family friend.

She'd been practicing for several years and her performance should be perfected by now. However, convincing herself she had no feelings for him was much easier when she didn't have to face him.

Now she had no choice. He was Adam's partner at the ranch and had been for the past twelve years. The ranch was the logical place for her to begin her search for her brother. And search for him she would. He was all she had.

The Fasten Seat Belts—No Smoking sign flashed on and Felicia hastily checked her hair and makeup in her small compact mirror. The face staring back at her looked considerably different from that of the naive young woman who had left the state five years before, convinced her heart was broken because Dane Rineholt didn't love her and had no desire to marry her.

Her sun-streaked blond hair was fashionably shaped in a long, straight bob that cupped under at the shoulders, framing her face. Felicia quickly ran a comb through it. The expensive cut was a far cry from the casual, unkempt style of her early years, when her biggest joy had been racing across the countryside on her horse, Blaze, the wind whipping her hair into a wild tangle.

Now she could look back on that young girl with pity for her dreams of marrying Dane and staying on the ranch, continuing to be a part of its expansion.

They had needed Dane's money and expertise to hang on to the ranch. She and Adam had worked hard to keep it. The St. Clair ranch had been in the same family for almost a hundred years, since the earliest settlers followed the trail from Galveston up to central Texas, settling near the Llano River in what was now Mason County.

A continued drought and poor beef prices had almost caused a twenty-year-old Adam to give up hope by the time Dane came along and offered to invest much needed capital into the place. His offer had been an answer to prayer. Looking back, Felicia could hardly blame Dane when the young girl she had been had seen him as their savior.

Felicia shook her head. No. Dane wasn't responsible for the way she felt about him. Her feelings were her problem, a problem she'd been working on for some time. She had been certain that eventually she would get over him. Once she was over him, she could be around him once again and treat him with the casual friendliness he deserved. However, she wasn't ready to see him now, not when her emotions were so raw because of Adam. She needed time to come to terms with all that had happened.

At least she had a few more hours before she would have to face Dane. She hadn't told him she was coming. Instead she'd reserved a rental car to be picked up at the airport. The drive to the ranch would give her time to prepare for their meeting.

Would Dane recognize the well-dressed, young executive as the young girl who had followed him and Adam around the ranch for years? She sincerely hoped not. Felicia hoped that young girl had been put away with all of the foolish dreams she'd once had.

Gathering her coat and purse, she moved with the passengers as they left the plane and followed the curving jetway into the Austin terminal. With a sinking heart, she spotted Dane as soon as she reached the doorway to the terminal. He wasn't hard to spot. Dane stood head and shoulders above the rest of the crowd waiting to greet the disembarking passengers.

How had he known she'd be on that plane? For that matter, how had he even known she would be coming? She hadn't said anything to him when he'd called. His news had left her so shaken she had scarcely been able to think. She barely remembered hanging up the phone.

Dane's piercing gaze met hers over the crowd and she mentally acknowledged that, like it or not, she now had to deal with the feelings he stirred within her every time she saw him. His steel-gray eyes seemed to see deep inside her, reading her thoughts and sensing her emotions. That ability to impale her with his gaze had many times kept her from getting into trouble as a young, high-spirited girl. He'd always seemed to know when she was even considering doing something Adam had forbidden her to do. Dane's added years had given him an air of authority that she had never dared to flout, even at her most rebellious stages.

She knew he wouldn't approve of her plans now to search for Adam, but many things had changed. She was twenty-seven years old, a mature woman, and she was going to do what she had to do in order to find her brother.

Felicia was swept along with the jostling passengers until she reached Dane. His impassive gaze never wavered when she paused in front of him. Whatever his thoughts, he kept them well hidden. Whatever emotions were stirred by seeing her after an absence of five years were his own very private feelings.

She fought the urge to throw herself into his arms like a child needing to be comforted. Instead she asked the question that had run through her mind in an endless refrain during the flight.

"Have you heard anything from Adam?"

He shook his head, lightly grasping her arm just above the elbow and piloting her down the concourse to the baggage claim area. "Nothing."

With one touch, Dane took control—of her and of the situation. The years seemed to drop away and once again she was following his lead. Felicia shook her head to dispel the sensation. Neither one of them was the same person. She had changed and grown. She needed to remember that. No doubt there were many changes in Dane, as well.

"How did you know I was coming in?"

He glanced down at her from the corner of his eye, keeping the rapid pace he'd set. With a slight quirk of his well-shaped mouth he murmured, "I've known you a long time, Felicia," as though that explained everything.

Perhaps it did.

"Does anybody have any idea what might have happened to him?" she asked, returning to the subject of Adam.

"The authorities have spoken to the personnel at the hotel in Monterrey where Adam generally stays. No one could pinpoint the exact time he was last seen there." He guided her out of the way of a woman pushing a luggage cart, gripping her arm more firmly. She could feel the warmth of his hand through her blouse, suit jacket and winter coat. "I talked with him last Friday and he said he intended to return home no later than Monday morning, which was yesterday. As I explained on the phone, when he didn't show up, I called down there and discovered he hadn't slept in his room since Thursday night."

They both were silent as they considered possible explanations.

"Why had he gone to Mexico?" Felicia finally asked.

"On business," was Dane's terse reply.

"Ranching?"

"He and I have several interests other than ranching."

"Oh. I didn't know."

"No," he agreed.

His response emphasized the strained relationship between them and she didn't know what to say. Felicia had deliberately cut herself off from any knowledge of the ranch in general and Dane Rineholt in particular during the past few years. She could hardly complain now that she didn't know anything about his and Adam's shared activities.

Slight chills ran through her body as a sudden gust of cold air eddied through the building from an open doorway somewhere. She knew the wind wasn't entirely to blame for her feeling of unease. Felicia had counted on the next few hours alone, but her time had run out. She now had to face Dane, inform him of her plans and face his predictable opposition.

While they stood waiting for her luggage to appear at the baggage claim area, Felicia could not help but notice the admiring glances from females that Dane's tall, lean figure drew. He'd had that effect on women as long as she'd known him.

His fleece-lined denim jacket clung to his shoulders, emphasizing their breadth, then narrowed to his flat, slim waist. Long, muscled legs were outlined by snug Levi's that had seen more than one washing. He didn't need the added height his custom-made boots gave him.

Dane Rineholt was the epitome of the Texas rancher. He wore his clothes with comfort and an unself-conscious ease. With a wry, inner amusement Felicia knew that Dane would be astonished to learn of the many restless nights she'd spent thinking about him. He took his style, his looks and his talents for granted.

Even in February his face was deeply tanned, except for the line on his forehead caused by wearing his Stetson whenever he was out of doors. He held the hat loosely in his hand, impatiently slapping it against his hard thigh as he watched for her luggage.

"How many bags do you have?"

"Two."

One brow lifted slightly, but he didn't say anything.

"I didn't expect to see you here," she finally said.

"Didn't you?" His sardonic response surprised her. "I knew you wouldn't take my advice and stay in L.A. This was the first flight you could have caught after I called."

She glanced down at the tips of her pumps. "I didn't realize I was so predictable."

One corner of his mouth lifted slightly. "You are to me."

Felicia didn't like the sound of that at all.

Dane Rineholt had always known more about her than she'd wanted him to know. She had hoped that as she'd grown older she had learned to hide what she was thinking and feeling. Of course Dane knew how close she was to Adam, so his ability to guess her actions wasn't too surprising.

She was an adult now, she reminded herself, one of the editors of a prestigious women's magazine. She had a life of her own, a career of her own. What more could she possibly want from life?

Dane's hand in the small of her back made her start and she quickly glanced up at him.

He nodded toward the baggage carousel. "You'll have to point out which ones are yours," he said in his husky drawl.

Moving closer to the conveyer belt, Felicia recognized that the deep vibrancy of Dane's voice had been one of the hardest things for her to forget. When she'd heard him on the phone the night before she immediately knew that she had not been successful. The velvet quality of his voice continued to wrap around her insides and tug incessantly at her heart. Felicia wryly admitted to herself that she carried a traitor in her bosom.

Placing his Stetson on his head, he picked up her two pieces of luggage as though they were empty and headed toward the door. Felicia followed reluctantly.

She thought of her intended rental car and regretted the loss of freedom a car would have given her. Instead she would have to borrow whatever was available at the ranch to drive to Mexico.

Of course, there was always the chance that by the time they reached the ranch Adam might have called, laughingly explaining his delay and apologizing for the scare. She would be able to handle the next few hours with Dane much easier if she knew such a message would be waiting when they got there.

Dane set her luggage down by the door while he studied the blowing rain. ''Wait here while I bring the car around.''

He didn't glance at her, but thrust the door open and strode toward the parking area, arrogantly knowing she would obey.

Felicia smiled slightly at the memories his tone of voice provoked. She could well remember several times when she had gone out of her way to resist his commands. What a pain she must have been. Yet he had been tolerant of her moods, much to her adolescent disgust. Felicia had unconsciously looked for ways to cause Dane to lose his grip on his self-control. She wondered if he'd been aware of her motives at the time.

A picture of Adam flashed in her mind and she knew he would be amused to think of them together without him around to referee. *Oh, Adam, please be all right,* she thought with a pang. Felicia could see him so well—the way he looked the last time he'd flown out to visit—his broad shoulders and slim hips causing her colleagues to take a second look.

Adam was good-looking, there was no doubt about it. They shared the same gray-green eyes, though his hair was tawnier than hers. His body showed that he spent his days in hard, physical labor. She was so proud of him, loved him so much, and could think of nothing that would have pleased her more than to see his mischievous grin teasing her about her quick temper and independent nature.

A late-model automobile drew up at the doors and Dane stepped out, moving with unconscious grace as he grabbed her bags and placed them in the trunk while she hurriedly climbed into the passenger's seat.

"This isn't a very good advertisement for the sunny South," Felicia said lightly when he slid into the driver's seat once more.

"We need the rain," he stated as they pulled away from the curb.

"That's what Adam said last time he called. Even the deer have been suffering."

Dane glanced over at her. "When did you speak with him last?"

She thought back. "About two weeks ago. Why?"

"Just wondered."

"What's going on, Dane?" she asked quietly.

"What do you mean?"

"You know more than you're telling about Adam's disappearance."

"Now what's your vivid imagination cooking up, tadpole?" he asked, amusement evident in his tone.

Tadpole. How she had hated that nickname. At a time when she was trying so hard to be an adult, trying to overcome the awkwardness of her too tall, too thin body, Dane had begun to call her by that irritating epithet.

"Adam wouldn't just disappear down there like some novice tourist. He has friends scattered throughout Mexico. What was he doing down there in the first place?"

She saw a grim expression settle over Dane's features. His firm jaw tightened for a moment, and she watched a tiny muscle pulse in his cheek.

"There's no reason for you to get involved, Felicia. You have your own life out on the West Coast. Hopefully Adam will turn up in a day or two and all this will be forgotten. Then you can fly back to your own world."

Felicia let her eyes focus back on the rapidly moving windshield wipers, not ready to get into that particular argument. She was glad after all that she wasn't the one having to drive. Visibility was poor. The streets and highway were flooded, unable to handle the sudden, fierce downpours that periodically hit the area.

Yet she felt safe. Dane had always made her feel that she could depend on him, even when she was the most irritated by his autocratic manner. When she was younger sometimes she had felt smothered by his and Adam's protectiveness. Now she felt rather comforted by it, which surprised her.

Resting her head wearily against the cushioned headrest, Felicia allowed her eyes to drift closed. She hadn't been able to sleep much. Her mind had been in a whirl since Dane's phone call the night before.

She'd known as soon as she heard his voice that something was wrong. Dane never called her. They had not been in touch with each other since she'd left Texas five years before. She had invariably used the excuse that her job kept her too busy to take time off so that Adam had always flown out to see her. She and Adam had never discussed her reasons for postponing her return to Texas, even for a short visit. Felicia had a hunch Adam had known. If he had, he never brought it up, just as he rarely mentioned Dane's name around her.

Oh, Adam. Where are you? Please don't be hurt somewhere, or sick. I love you so much. Please take care of yourself.

The rhythmic swish of the wipers lulled her into a restless sleep.

* * *

Fifteen-year-old Felicia St. Clair stepped off the school bus that had paused at the end of the lane leading up to the ranch house. A hot breeze caused a dust swirl to greet her, making her feel even hotter and stickier.

How she hated Texas. The heat, the dirt, Adam's constant concern over water and the state of the cattle. He was too young to have to deal with the responsibility of the multiacre ranch. When her mother had died three years ago, Adam had assumed full responsibility of the ranch and all its headaches at the ripe old age of seventeen.

She sometimes wondered how he stood it. Of course Pete had been there to guide Adam and help him. Otherwise Adam would never have managed the two years of college at Texas A & M, driving home every weekend to help where he could. Even that proved too much, and Adam hadn't bothered to go back this year.

Pete had been their father's foreman, and had stayed on these fifteen years, looking after the ranch and his best friend's family. Pete and Jim St. Clair had met during the war.

When it was over Jim had convinced Pete there was a need for him there in Texas on the ranch.

Felicia sometimes wondered if it wouldn't have been better if her mother had sold the ranch when her father had died, instead of trying to keep it going. Adam could remember their father and his dreams for the place. As far back as she could recall, all Adam could talk about, think about or dream about was how he intended to fulfill his father's dreams. And he'd had Pete there to help him.

Adam had grown up too fast. He'd never had a chance to be a carefree boy. Instead he'd taken over the task of caring for his widowed mother and sister with determined zeal.

After their mother had died, he'd hired a housekeeper to look after them. Millie was a warm, comfortable person who'd done all she could to make the orphaned teenagers feel like they had a family.

Felicia gripped her schoolbooks tighter and began the long walk to the house.

Lately Adam had spent his evenings poring over the account books. There had been little moisture the previous winter and she knew he was worried.

Felicia's daydreams carried her far away from the dusty tracks leading to the ranch buildings. She was a famous writer living in a spacious, penthouse apartment in some large city. Sometimes she was in New York. Other times, Paris, London, Rome, Athens. Always she was surrounded by people who toasted and applauded her. She saw herself dressed in silks and satins, furs and jewelry, never in chambray, denim and worn boots.

Her English teacher had returned her essay that day and had quietly praised her work, giving Felicia more fuel to create fantasies for her future.

She was busily trying to decide how much money she would send to Adam each month for the ranch so he could make the necessary improvements that seemed to worry him so, when Prince, a mongrel dog that had been around as far back as Felicia could remember, came bounding up to her, barking ecstatically.

"Oh, Prince, you fool. Get down. You'd think I'd been gone for years." She was laughing at his antics. For an old dog he could certainly show youthful enthusiasm at times.

She was walking backward, scolding him, which was why she didn't see Adam and the stranger standing on the porch watching her, until she turned around to start up the steps.

Felicia knew everybody in Mason County, at least everyone who made his home there. And she knew very well she had never laid eyes on this man before.

He was several inches taller than Adam, but they were built along similar lines: broad shoulders, slim waist and hips, long legs. They were even dressed similarly, in light-weight shirts of blue chambray. But where Adam's open, humorous expression made him look even younger than his twenty years, the stranger had a closed expression on his face, his eyes slitted against the bright sunlight, his hat pulled down low over the bridge of his nose. He seemed considerably older than Adam.

Felicia felt all knees and elbows as she gazed up at the man leaning gracefully against the porch rail. She had a sudden vision of herself as she must look to him, tall and angular, her blond hair pulled away from her face by over-size hair clips and falling over her shoulders in careless disarray.

A hollow place seemed to form somewhere just below her ribs and she unconsciously placed her hand there, wondering what it was about the stranger that had suddenly made her aware of what she looked like. She had never cared before.

"Hi, Sis," Adam said with a casual grin. "I want you to meet Dane Rineholt."

Glancing over at the man who had neither changed expression nor position, Felicia tentatively smiled. "H'lo."

Adam continued with the introduction. "Dane, this is my sister, Felicia." He dropped his arm around her shoulders and hugged her close. "She's one of the best ranch hands we've got."

She glanced under her lashes at her brother. "I'm the *only* ranch hand you've got, besides Pete," she pointed out.

"Well, that's going to change. Dane has agreed to become a partner on the ranch. He's already made some suggestions that will free both of us from some of our duties."

Felicia stared in shock at the other man. What did Adam mean, a partner? "You mean you are now part owner of the St. Clair ranch?"

Dane slowly straightened to his full height. In a voice that seemed to rumble from his broad chest, he answered, "That's right." The tone made it clear the subject wasn't open to debate.

Felicia could feel her heart racing. Her life had been fairly structured, the days blending together into a seamless whole of helping Adam with the morning chores, going to school, coming home and helping Millie with the household chores. She had a sudden instinctive feeling that nothing in her life would be the same again.

She glanced at her brother. "Does that mean he's going to live with us?" she asked in a low voice.

A sudden, slashing smile caused Dane's face to take on an entirely different look. The brackets that formed on either side of his mouth indicated what might have been dimples on a woman. On him they looked like deep slash marks. The sudden gleam of white in his sun-darkened face made an astonishing difference. Felicia could only stare at the transformation.

"That's what it means, all right. But you don't need to worry. I'm no threat to a tadpole like you, honey. You'll be perfectly safe around me."

She could feel the color flood her face and for a moment she wished she could shrink to invisibility. His teasing tone made it clear he meant nothing by the remark, but she felt as though her errant thoughts about him must have betrayed her in some way. Felicia wished she had the necessary sophistication to respond to his banter in an equally careless fashion. Unfortunately her brain had clogged and she could think of nothing to say.

Adam compounded her embarrassment by laughing at her chagrin. "She's a little shy, Dane. Not used to being around people very much."

How could he? Adam made her sound as though she had been hidden somewhere out on the back forty, with no training whatsoever.

Felicia raised her chin, forcing her eyes to meet the dancing steel-gray ones almost hidden under the brim of his hat. "It isn't that I'm shy exactly, Mr. Rineholt. I just don't know what to say to someone so much older. My mother always taught me to show respect to my elders."

The sparkle in Dane's eyes was only increased by her provocative statement. "Oh, I'm not so old that I don't understand when

I'm being baited. You'll be surprised at how much younger I'll appear to you in another few years.''

Adam dropped his arm from her shoulders, patted her awkwardly and said, ''You run on inside now, honey. I know Millie's been hoping you would help her with her canning today. We'll see you later.''

Felicia watched as the two men left the porch, Dane lightly touching the brim of his hat with his finger in a subtle acknowledgment of her. She had always thought Adam was tall because he was over six feet, but Dane must have been at least four inches taller than Adam.

She couldn't seem to stop staring at the man as he walked beside Adam, his casual grace unstudied, his catlike stride causing the hollow place in her stomach to glow with an unfamiliar sensation.

Felicia had never seen another man like him.

By the time she was a senior in high school, two years later, Felicia knew there would never be another man in her life to compare with Dane Rineholt.

She couldn't understand the flurry of confused emotions that came over her whenever he was around. Felicia even dreamed about him occasionally, much to her embarrassment and chagrin. She hated being so aware of him and tried to cover up her reactions whenever he was around.

Not that her behavior toward him seemed to matter. Dane treated her the same way Adam did, with a casual familiarity that Felicia found insulting coming from him. In fact, she bristled at everything he said and did. Particularly the odious nickname that he continued to use. Tadpole. How revolting.

Perhaps she had been in the transition between child and adult when he'd first met her, but two years had brought about several changes in her appearance. Slowly but surely the angular parts of her body had begun to fill out, becoming firm and rounded. She and her girlfriends experimented with cosmetics, taking turns practicing on one another, until she found a style that was comfortable and becoming to her.

Her mirror told Felicia that she was not ugly. Wide-spaced gray-green eyes stared back at her, framed by long, thick lashes. High cheekbones gave her face an elegant shape that her friends good-naturedly envied. And her tanned skin made the light color of blond hair even more noticeable.

The boys at school had taken to hanging around the ranch in their spare time, which was little enough, because they, too, had work that needed to be done at home.

Adam enjoyed teasing her about her following, but Dane never said a word. He just sat there watching her with an inner amusement that irritated her beyond belief.

Sometimes she would lie awake at night and dream of the time when she'd be rich and famous and he'd come to visit, to beg her to marry him, to swear his undying love for her, and she would laugh in his face. Somehow she could never see him bowed and broken, even in her imagination. But she could pretend to see pain in his eyes, pretend that he loved her desperately and couldn't bear to let her go.

But in the light of day, all she ever encountered was the amused mockery in his eyes.

Until the night Blaze was sick.

Dane's presence in their lives and in the running of the ranch had made a considerable difference. There was money enough to buy more stock, including horses, as well as hire additional help. Although Felicia still helped with the house, she was no longer asked to work on the ranch.

And when one of the mares had a colt, Adam had allowed her to keep it.

She never gave up her dreams of leaving Texas and becoming a writer. In fact, she still spent hours writing, filling pages with imaginary characters, her men always having a steely-gray gaze. Yet she also enjoyed being outdoors and working with the horses. Especially Blaze.

So when he became ill she was beside herself.

"I don't think it's anything too serious." Pete tried to comfort her in his usual, taciturn way. "Probably ate something that didn't agree with him."

She hoped he was right, but she didn't want to take any chances. She made preparations to spend the night in the barn so that she would be nearby in case he became worse. She was kneeling beside the horse, murmuring softly, when she looked up to see Dane standing near the stall.

"I don't see any reason for you to stay out here tonight, tadpole. Blaze is looking considerably better than he was earlier."

Sleepily she glanced up at the man, his height even more noticeable from her present position. "He seems to rest easier when I'm here. Every time I get up he starts stirring."

"You're spoiling that damned horse, you know."

"I don't care."

"He's not going to be worth much to anyone around here."

"I don't care."

Dane knelt down beside her. "That horse is all you care about, isn't it?"

She glanced up at him, startled. "Of course not. I care about Adam and Millie and Pete. And you," she added slowly.

He grinned. "Well, I'm glad I made your list, anyway. Sometimes it's hard to tell with you."

"Well, if you didn't tease me so much, I'd probably be a lot nicer to you."

"Tadpole, if I didn't tease you, then you'd know I don't like you."

"See what I mean? How many times have I asked you not to call me 'tadpole'?"

"The reason you're so much fun to tease is that you always react, didn't anyone ever tell you that?'' Dane shifted, sitting down on the straw beside her.

"Did anyone ever tease you?" she asked, stroking Blaze's neck.

"Are you kidding? With two older brothers? It's a wonder I ever survived with those two around. Their teasing could become painfully physical at times."

"I didn't know you had any family, Dane."

"What did you think? That I'd been hatched from an egg?"

She glanced around at him out of the corner of her eye. "Yeah. A lizard egg."

"Tacky, tacky. And here I thought we were getting along so well for a change." He chuckled.

"Tell me about your family. You never seem to talk about your life before you came here."

"That's because there was nothing much to talk about. My folks own a ranch south of San Antonio. I have two younger sisters besides my brothers. After college I went into the service, came back and worked with my dad for a while, then decided I needed to be on my own, so I headed north."

"You still aren't on your own, staying here with us."

"But Adam needed some help. He's got a good place here, but you've been through some lean years. I was asking about possible ranch land for sale in town, when I heard about the St. Clair place. Someone mentioned that Adam might be willing to sell, so I thought I'd make him an offer."

"And he told you he didn't want to sell."

"That was understandable. But I liked him. He's young but settled, determined and a hard worker, the kind of person you'd want on your side if the going ever got tough."

"I know. I'm fortunate to have him."

"That you are."

"How old are you, Dane?"

He lifted one brow slightly. "How old do you think I am?"

She studied him for a moment. Trying to restrain her smile, she offered, "Oh, forty or so."

He grabbed her by the shoulders and lightly shook her, causing her to chuckle at his mock ferocious expression. "You know better than that. I haven't reached thirty yet."

"But you're still years older than I am."

"Ten years."

"Ancient."

"But well preserved," he offered with a grin.

She continued to study him as he slowly let his hands leave her shoulders. "I suppose. Some people might find you attractive."

"Some people, but not you, I take it?"

"For an old man you aren't too bad."

He threw back his head and laughed, and she grinned, pleased to see that he could take her kidding in good fun. After a few minutes, she said in a quiet voice, "Thank you for checking on us tonight."

"No problem. Look. He's doing much better. Why don't we go back to the house?" He stood and pulled her up beside him. Blaze never stirred and Felicia admitted to herself that he seemed much better. Dane still held her hand, his rough callused fingers gripping hers firmly. Obediently she followed him out of the stall and they crossed the area between the barn and the house in silence.

A full moon cast mysterious shadows over the area, making the plain, ordinary ranch yard seem different, almost enchanted. Felicia paused, gazing up at the sky with a pleasurable sense of belonging.

Her view of the sky was suddenly blocked by a shadow as Dane slowly leaned down and kissed her softly on the lips. Pulling back slightly, he said in a low voice, "You look like a fairy princess standing here bathed in silver light. I couldn't resist."

She stared at him in wonder. Although Adam was affectionate with her, hugging her at various times, he wasn't one to touch her often, so she wasn't used to it. The boys she knew treated her more as a pal than a female. Surprised at the intimacy from Dane, she realized that he had just given her her first kiss.

She touched her lips with her fingers and gazed up at him in amazement.

"I'm sorry. I didn't mean to offend you."

"You didn't offend me," she managed to say. "You just surprised me."

"I take it you aren't used to being kissed."

She stiffened at the amusement she could hear in his voice. "On the contrary," she said loftily. "I'm just not used to *you* kissing me, that's all."

Felicia was glad he couldn't know how her heart raced at the moment. It increased its rate when he pulled her into his arms and said,

"Oh, then you won't mind if I kiss you again, since you're used to being kissed."

Before she could frame a reply, his mouth had found hers once more. However, this kiss was considerably different from the first one. This time his arms were firmly around her, pulling her close to his hard body. There was no tentative touch with this one. His mouth felt hard and firm and she gasped with surprise.

Taking advantage of her parted lips, he ran his tongue along the uneven edge of her teeth, lightly forcing his way.

Felicia couldn't think. Sensations she never knew existed swept over her. She felt hot and cold at the same time and her knees would not have supported her weight. But she needn't have worried. Dane stood with his legs braced, holding her against him as he slowly explored the depths of her mouth.

Feeling the urge to touch him, Felicia placed her hands around his waist and began smoothing the material that covered his muscled back. In the years since he'd been at the ranch she'd seen him many times without a shirt, his back as dark as the rest of him. But never before had she had the opportunity to feel the rippling muscles. Until now.

She could feel his heart pounding in his chest, the thudding shaking them both. And she realized that this was better than any of the fantasies she had made up during the nights she couldn't sleep.

Dane's hand moved slowly up and down her spine as though memorizing it, from the curve of her neck, over her shoulders, down to her waist and then her hips. A tingling sensation followed everywhere he touched and she found herself wanting to get closer to him somehow. She moaned slightly, unaware that she did so.

Dane lifted his head abruptly, as though the sound had broken his concentration. She never knew for sure why he stopped, only that he did. She couldn't see his eyes because his face was in shadow. The moonlight fell full on her upturned countenance and she knew he must be able to tell by her expression what she was feeling.

"I'm sorry, Felicia. I shouldn't have done that."

Appalled to hear him apologizing for something so marvelous, she stared up at him in silence.

"You have every right to be angry at me. I don't know what I was thinking of." He shook his head as though trying to clear it, meanwhile stepping away from her, leaving at least two feet of space between them.

"You don't have to apologize," she managed to mutter. "It's okay."

"I'm old enough to know better." He looked around as though trying to remember what they were doing out there at that time of night. "You better get some sleep. You have school in the morning."

"I know. You don't have to remind me."

"I'll see you tomorrow, then." He turned to walk away, heading back toward the barn, then paused. Glancing at her, he said, "I promise I won't do that again, tadpole. I never meant to take advantage of you."

"You didn't."

He shrugged. "Good night."

Felicia spent a very restless night, trying to come to grips with the feelings Dane had invoked in her, trying not to feel rejected because of his actions after the kiss. One thing she knew. She would have to hide her feelings for Dane even more so now than in the past. She couldn't bear to have him make fun of her, which she was sure he would do if he thought she cared for him. He still saw her as a child.

Felicia no longer felt like a child. Dane's kiss had released her from the warm cocoon of her childhood into the burning ache of adult emotions.

Two

After the night that Dane kissed her, Felicia was constantly aware of him. He, on the other hand, seemed to have forgotten she existed. Where he used to spend his evenings with her and Adam, reading or watching television, he now seemed to have interests elsewhere, often leaving directly after supper to make the long drive into town.

She couldn't understand why Dane was suddenly so busy, but she hesitated to discuss the change with Adam. He might wonder why she was so interested in Dane's schedule. Or worse. He might think she was harboring a crush for Dane.

During one of those evenings, Adam brought up the subject of college. "Do you have any idea where you want to go?" he asked, after she had mentioned that several representatives from various colleges had presented a program at school that day.

"I think I'd like to go to the university in Austin," she admitted.

"You traitor," he responded with a grin. The rivalry between the University of Texas and Texas A & M was legendary and was carried long past college days.

"They have a great journalism department," she pointed out patiently.

"But how will I ever be able to face our friends?"

"You don't have to act as though I've gone into a house of prostitution, you know."

Adam laughed. "All right, you win. It will be nice to have you close by, I have to admit."

"Yes. Maybe I can even find a friend while I'm there who might be interested in meeting my older brother."

"None of that now. I have no intention of getting married. You know that."

"But that's silly."

"I have enough responsibility without adding more."

"But I won't always be a responsibility."

"I wasn't referring to you. You, my dear sister, have been a reward."

Her eyes misted over and she walked over to where he sat and hugged him. "That's the nicest thing you've ever said to me."

He hugged her back fiercely. "I mean it. There were times that having you was the only thing that kept me going."

"Well, when I'm a rich and famous writer you won't have to work so hard. I'll send you all the money you could possibly want."

"Rich and famous, huh? Not that I doubt you in the least, but I don't think I'll start spending it right now, if you don't mind." He stood up and stretched. "In fact, I think I'll turn in. Five o'clock comes mighty early in the morning."

He wandered out of the room and she heard him in the kitchen. He was probably snitching another piece of the cake that Millie had baked for supper.

Felicia wasn't sleepy. She was restless and on edge. Where had Dane gone these past few weeks? And why did she get the distinct impression he was avoiding her?

She was still reading in the living room hours later, when she heard Dane's pickup truck pull up outside. She heard the truck door quietly close, as though he were trying not to make noise, then his soft steps crossing the front porch. The screen door opened with a protesting creak.

He paused in the hallway and she looked up from her book, determined not to let him know she had been listening for him. He stood in the shadowed doorway, watching her in silence.

"Hello, Dane," she finally said, softly.

"It's a little late for you to be up, isn't it?" His voice sounded harsh in the quiet night.

She bristled slightly. "I already have a brother, you know. I don't need another one."

He muttered something under his breath that sounded suspiciously like a curse. Perhaps it was better she hadn't heard what he'd said. Then he walked into the room.

"You don't have to be so damned defensive, Felicia. I was just making conversation."

She tilted her head slightly, studying him as he moved into the light of the lamp beside her chair. His hair was rumpled and there was a stain around his mouth that looked suspiciously like lipstick.

"It's a little late for you to be up, too, as far as that goes," she said stiffly.

"I think I can handle it."

"I'm sure you can." Felicia glanced down at the book she held in her hand. She hadn't the foggiest idea what it was about. She'd been sitting there staring at the pages for hours, waiting for him to come home.

With newfound resolve, Felicia stood and faced Dane as much as possible, taking into account the fact that he was almost a foot taller than she was. "Are you angry at me for some reason?"

One brow lifted quizzically. "Of course not. Why do you ask?"

"You've been treating me differently."

"That's your imagination."

"Is it?"

"Of course."

"You know, Dane," she tried for a light tone, "that color lipstick really doesn't do much for you. It's not your shade."

He stood there, looking down at her without changing expression. "I'm not worried about it."

"I'm sure you're not."

"Why don't you go to bed?"

"Why don't you stop telling me what to do?"

His sigh was full of exasperation. "I'll be glad when you grow up," he muttered.

"Funny. The way you kissed me a few weeks ago gave me the impression you thought I was."

He chuckled. "Not hardly. Your innocence was showing, tadpole. That wasn't much of a kiss."

She could feel her temper rising as he stood there with a half smile on his face. He was so smug. He knew very well what he looked like, his thick, black hair falling across his forehead. No doubt the woman he'd been with had left him in no doubt as to his desirability.

She stepped closer. "Well, I've been practicing. Is this any better?"

Before he could say anything she slid her arms around his neck and went up on tiptoe, pulling his head down to meet hers. She touched his cool, firm lips with her tongue, stroking it lightly over his top lip, then gradually caressing his fuller lower lip.

He grabbed both of her forearms as though intending to pull away from her. She merely tightened her grip around his neck, moving closer so that her body was fully aligned with his.

She could feel his tension and the muscles in his neck tighten as he attempted to raise his head. Then she placed her lips on his and, imitating his previous actions, inserted her tongue between his lips.

Her initial reason for kissing him was out of frustrated anger, but as soon as her mouth touched his, she forgot her anger and his evasiveness and instead enjoyed the touch, taste and scent of him. His after-shave reminded her of piny woods and outdoor breezes and she paused for a moment, inhaling, before she continued her foray.

The actual kiss was better than her memories had been and she relaxed against him, confident of his ability not to let her fall as she coaxed him into a response.

Dane took over the kiss, sweeping her off her feet. He strode over to the chair she had been in and sat down with her draped across his lap while he continued to kiss her.

If their first kiss could be classified in the grade-school category, this kiss skipped right into higher education.

Dane treated her as though she were experienced, kissing her with a possessiveness that left her breathless. His mouth roamed over her face, his lips touching her eyes, her cheeks, then nibbling around her ear.

And his hands weren't idle. His large hand cupped itself around her breast, his thumb gently rubbing the peak until she thought she would scream with the sensation. She couldn't be still. The fires that he had started within her caused her to squirm restlessly in his lap until he held her solidly against him and muttered, "Stop that! You don't have any idea what you're asking for!"

His mouth returned to hers, sliding familiarly across her lips as though already at home there, his tongue slipping intimately within, touching and intertwining with hers, creating a mating ritual all its own.

Her hand rested lightly on his chest and she could feel the heavy thudding of his heart and hear his labored breathing. With a boldness she never knew she possessed, Felicia unfastened two of his buttons and slid her hand through the opening, enjoying the feel of his hair-roughened chest.

He felt so good, even better than her imaginings. She had no idea touching him would create so many enjoyable sensations deep inside of her.

"Oh, Felicia," he murmured a few minutes later, or was it hours? He rested his forehead against hers. "Don't do this to me. Please."

He was trembling and the hand that had rested on her breast lay, palm upward, in her lap.

"What am I doing?" she whispered.

"Driving me out of my mind," he admitted.

She laid her head on his shoulder. "I love you so much, Dane." She kept her face averted from him.

The silence of the room seemed to wrap around them and she realized that Dane had caught his breath at her words. Then she felt his chest move as he slowly exhaled, the sound halfway between a sigh and a groan.

"Tadpole, you have no earthly idea what you're talking about," he murmured, his hand absently stroking her spine.

Dismayed at his response, she raised her head and stared at him. "What do you mean?"

"What you're feeling at the moment, darlin', is not love. It's good old-fashioned lust, and believe me, the two are oftentimes confused."

"Then what is love?"

"A combination of things that I don't intend to go into at the moment. Even if you aren't tired, I am. I'm going to bed." He stood up as though she weighed little to nothing in his arms, placing her gently on her feet.

"I wish you'd stop treating me like a child, Dane," she complained.

"It's hard not to, when you're still a child in so many ways... in a very adult body. I'm not going to take advantage of that, no matter what the provocation."

He turned around and started out of the room, and she was left standing in the middle of the room, bewildered by the conflicting thoughts and feelings that ran through her.

* * *

The rain was getting worse, if anything, and Dane was forced to slow down even more for safety's sake. He glanced at the sleeping woman beside him.

He had honestly thought he was over her. After all, five years was a long time and there had been many women willing to take the place she had occupied in his mind and heart. When she continued to make excuses about why she couldn't come back to visit he'd known that whatever they had once shared had dissipated, at least on her part, over the years. So he had put her out of his head. Or so he thought.

Now he realized the foolishness in his thinking. Felicia St. Clair had made a place in his heart that was peculiarly her own and no one would ever be able to replace her.

He still remembered the first time he'd seen her. She couldn't have been more than fifteen years old, with a coltish quality about her he'd found instantly endearing.

She'd been walking up the lane from the county road, playing with the dog, laughing and teasing, her smile so radiant that it practically lit up the countryside.

He'd forgotten that there was such innocence in the world. After the years he'd spent
overseas, and later in his special investigative
field, he'd returned to Texas to make peace
with himself and to try to establish a quiet, ordinary life-style that would slowly give him
back his ability to enjoy life.

He had met with Adam St. Clair several
times, working on the partnership agreement,
before he finally saw Felicia. Adam had mentioned her more than once and it had been obvious there was a close bond between the two
of them, but for some reason Dane had pic-
tured a child.

When he and Adam had decided to go
ahead and form a partnership Adam seemed to
take it for granted that Dane would move in to
the old farmhouse. It was certainly large
enough to house several people, with its large
bedroom and bath downstairs, used by Millie,
and the four bedrooms upstairs.

He hadn't given much thought to what it
would mean to share the home of a young girl
slowly blossoming into womanhood. Until he
saw her that day.

The sun picked up glints of color from her
hair, making it shine silver. She'd been hot,

and soft curls had framed her face. She had stared up at him in surprise, and he would never forget the first glimpse of her eyes, their coloring so much like Adam's, their shape and expression so definitely her own.

They had reminded him of a fawn he'd once startled in the woods—wide eyed and wary, too young to know whether there was a reason to fear the newcomer. Her cheeks had bloomed with health beneath her Texas tan.

He glanced over at her now, concerned at the lack of color in those cheeks at the moment.

Could he blame her?

Knowing how close she was to Adam, he had known he couldn't keep her brother's disappearance from her. He had also known she wouldn't be able to stay away. After all, when Adam did show up—and Dane said a silent prayer that he was safe—the ranch would be the first place he'd come to or contact.

A frown appeared between Dane's brows. If there were only some kind of clue to follow. Adam knew that what he was doing was dangerous and Dane felt responsible for having recruited him. But when the authorities had contacted Dane and asked him to continue the work he had done for them overseas here in the States, he couldn't say no. Somebody had to do it, and the government had spent many thousands of dollars training him.

Adam had been a natural. He enjoyed the danger and intrigue, but didn't take unnecessary chances. In the four years they had been working with the government, they had managed to stop some major sources of drug smuggling between the States and Mexico.

Only now Dane was afraid Adam's luck had run out.

On the surface he was a typical tourist-businessman who mysteriously and with no apparent reason had disappeared while visiting a foreign country. But the covert authorities on both sides of the river knew his disappearance could have more sinister overtones. He wouldn't be the first agent to disappear and never be heard of again.

The question that Dane had wrestled with was what to tell Felicia. Adam had casually mentioned after one of his trips to L.A. that what they were doing had been made easier by the fact that Felicia was far enough away not to ask unanswerable questions. From his comment, Dane realized that Adam had taken his advice and not told her about their activities.

Now that Felicia was in Texas, Dane wondered if she would continue to accept the incident as some unexplained tourist disappearance. She hadn't pursued her questions earlier, but she could very well be saving them until they reached home. He felt so helpless, sitting there waiting for reports, but there was so little he could do.

Their contacts across the border had no idea he and Adam worked together. They had independently infiltrated unrelated drug operations, so he didn't know Adam's contacts in Mexico. He also knew that if some news didn't turn up in the next few days, he'd jeopardize his cover and go down there himself and use his own sources.

Felicia turning up complicated things in more ways than one.

Once again he glanced over at her. She was too thin. Probably didn't eat regular meals or was caught up in the slim-and-trim craze.

He would never forget how she'd looked a few weeks before she'd graduated from the university. At twenty-two she had become one of the loveliest women he'd ever seen.

For four years he had worked hard to give her the impression that he was serious about someone else so that she wouldn't practice her budding feminine wiles on him. She had caught him by surprise the spring she'd graduated from high school with her unexpected passionate response to him. He had quickly realized it was up to him to take control of the situation.

He lived with her and yet wasn't a relative. There was no way he'd betray Adam's trust by taking advantage of her innocence.

The situation improved somewhat after she left for college, even though she came home occasionally for a weekend. He planned his weekends so that he was seldom there when she was. Being away not only helped him maintain his self-control, it also gave Felicia and Adam an opportunity to spend time together.

After four years of that routine he'd been lulled into a sense of false security, until he'd felt there was no longer a problem. The tension between them seemed to have disappeared and once again he was able to adopt a casually friendly attitude toward her.

Then she had asked him to escort her to one of the graduation festivities, and like a fool he agreed to go.

He would remember that night for as long as he lived.

Adam had teased him about having a date with a girl young enough to be his daughter, which Dane had taken great exception to. He certainly hadn't been that precocious at ten years of age! But behind the teasing, Dane felt that Adam was curious about his willingness to take her.

Not that he hadn't tried to convince Felicia to go with someone her own age. But she had insisted that she wasn't dating anyone at the moment. She wouldn't have an escort if he didn't take her, and she refused to attend alone.

So he agreed to take her. Adam didn't ask any questions, but Dane knew him well enough to know he had some. Dane, though, had never been able to discuss his feelings for Felicia with anyone, not even her own brother. Or perhaps especially not with her own brother.

He felt ashamed of his strong physical reaction toward her. After all, she was little more than a child. He had helped to raise her, or at least he felt that way at times.

And he was too old for her. Much too old. From everything Adam had said over the years, Felicia was counting the days before she could leave the ranchland behind and spend her life in the city.

In the meantime he agreed to escort her to her party.

Dane showed up at her dorm at the appointed hour and he got his first glimpse of the woman she'd become while he wasn't looking.

She took his breath away.

Felicia wore a floor-length gown of the softest blue-green he'd ever seen. The color reminded him of the ocean on a calm, sunny day. Her eyes glittered, their color enhanced by an iridescent green underslip that shimmered through the sheer surface of the softly swirling material.

Her hair had been cut so that her natural waves turned into feathery curls framing her face, drawing attention to the patrician line of brow, high cheek bones and dainty nose.

She looked like a princess, and Dane knew he had been fighting a losing battle regarding his feelings for her.

Felicia smiled shyly at him. "I'm not used to seeing you so dressed up," she admitted, and he glanced down at the formal suit he wore.

"I don't think this would be appropriate for the ranch, do you?"

Her grin looked more natural as she responded to his teasing tone. "True."

"Shall we go?" he asked, trying to sound at ease.

She nodded in an unconsciously regal gesture.

Felicia seemed happy to have him there, and he tried to convince himself he was little more than a brother to her and not to take her obvious excitement for anything more than the knowledge that she would soon be through with school.

He lost track of the names and faces of the people she introduced him to that night, a little surprised that so many of her girlfriends made reference to having heard about him.

He and Felicia had never danced together before because they had never been in a social situation such as they were that night. He knew she expected him to be the perfect escort, and with something close to grim determination, Dane set out to fulfill her wishes.

He couldn't deny that he enjoyed holding her in his arms during the few numbers when the band hired for the occasion played something slow, but that created its own problems. He didn't know which was worse—holding her close to him and forcing his body not to react to her nearness, or watching her stand in front of him during the upbeat numbers, her face flushed and smiling, her body dipping and weaving in unconsciously provocative movements.

Dane felt relieved when Felicia suggested they leave.

They were in the car returning to her dorm when she asked, "Are you driving home tonight?"

"No. I'm staying at a motel."

"Oh." She was silent for a moment. "Will I see you again before you leave?"

"I hadn't planned on it. Why?"

She shrugged. "Just wondered."

He couldn't drop the subject. "Why? Did you want a ride home?"

"Oh, no. I still have another week at school before I can go home."

They lapsed back into silence.

"Are you hungry?" Dane asked finally, breaking the silence.

"A little."

"Would you like to get something to eat? I think I saw an all-night restaurant near the motel. Or do you have to be back right away?"

"I have plenty of time, Dane. I just don't want to delay you any more. I really do appreciate your coming to Austin to take me to the dance."

"Have you ever known me to deny you anything, tadpole?" he asked wryly.

The smile she gave him almost caused him to miss his turn.

Dane sat across from her during their meal, fascinated by her ever changing expressions as she told him hilarious tales of life in the dorm and on campus. She was so full of life and energy that he almost envied her that naive confidence that life was waiting for her in order to fulfill her every dream and expectation.

When they left the restaurant Felicia asked if he would show her his room. She explained that she'd never been inside a motel room.

"I find that hard to believe," he responded, reluctantly walking her across the parking area to the motel.

"It's true. Adam and I never traveled, so there was no reason for me to stay in one."

"And no man has ever coaxed you to one before?" he asked quizzically, opening the door of his room and stepping back to allow her to precede him into the room.

She grinned up at him. "I didn't say they haven't tried, Dane." Felicia walked past him through the open door.

His room was a standard style, with a king-size bed taking up a considerable amount of the space. A round table with two chairs were by the window and a sliding glass door spanned the width of the room. Felicia wandered over, parting the draperies slightly to take in the view.

"Oh, look. You have a pool!"

"That's not unusual. Most motels do."

She spun around with a mischievous sparkle in her eye. "I know! Why don't we go swimming?"

He sat down on the side of the bed, her youthful exuberance suddenly making him feel the weight of his added years. "Felicia, use your head. Neither of us brought anything to swim in."

Her gaze suddenly focused past his shoulders to the wall behind him. "Oh, look! You have a wall of mirrors. This is really fancy."

He was having trouble keeping up with her rapid subject changes.

Felicia walked past him into the bathroom, where she turned on the light, played with the fan switches, then reappeared. "I really feel like a country bumpkin. This is so modern compared to home."

"You have a very lovely home, tadpole. Don't ever be ashamed of it."

Her eyes widened with astonishment at his comment. "Oh, I'm not ashamed, Dane. I wouldn't want to change a thing about it. But I like this, too." She glanced back at the window, then at him. "Nobody would see us swimming now, you know. Couldn't we swim in our underwear? After all, that's more than you and Adam use at home."

"How the hell do you know what Adam and I swim in or don't swim in?"

"Because Adam's told me about you guys stripping down and swimming in the river on a hot day."

"Adam's got a big mouth."

She laughed. "Don't be so uptight, Dane. I promise I won't embarrass you by staring."

He studied her for a moment in silence, then slowly shook his head. "I don't think Adam would approve."

She must have heard something in his voice that told her he was weakening. The thought had crossed his mind that it would be fun on a hot night to cool off in the pool. She disappeared into the bathroom. "I'll keep a towel around me in case anyone is watching. Come on, Dane. It'll be fun."

She had echoed his thoughts and he decided that he didn't have to play parent with her— she was a grown woman.

While she was slipping out of her formal, he quickly undressed, finding a pair of Levi's to wear, so that when she reappeared, demurely draped by an oversized towel, he silently opened the sliding glass door that gave them direct access to the pool and stepped outside.

The night was hot and muggy, typical of Texas in late spring. Indirect lighting gave a soft glow to the pool area and Dane admitted the idea of a midnight swim held considerable appeal.

He unfastened his jeans and pulled them off, revealing the navy blue briefs he wore, which could pass for swimming trunks.

Felicia tossed her towel on a nearby chair and walked over to the steps leading into the water.

Dane had to admit there was nothing childish about the body revealed to him. The lacy underwear she had on was probably more than adequate for today's swimwear styles, but Dane had not seen her in a swimsuit in several years. Gone were the coltish lines. In their place was a slender young woman with curving breasts and thighs, and a waist that made him want to wrap his hands around it.

He forced himself to look away, waiting until he heard the sounds of water rippling as she splashed around.

"Come on in," she said gaily, "the water feels great. It's nice and warm."

Dane didn't need nice and warm at the present. A Swedish dip would have been much more appropriate. It occurred to him that a midnight swim would have been fine if Adam had been along. But he wasn't. There were just the two of them. Perhaps Felicia saw him as another brother, but the feelings churning inside him were anything but brotherly. A midnight swim with Felicia was certainly not one of his better ideas.

At first he stayed the pool length away from her, swimming laps to keep his mind off her and how she looked in the moonlight.

Eventually she came gliding through the water to join him at the deep end of the pool.

"Don't you ever just relax and enjoy the water?" she asked, a hint of laughter in her voice. "You act as though you're training for the Olympics!"

He ran his hand through his hair, shoving it out of his face and flicking water over them both. "Just getting rid of some excess energy."

"I see," she said with a nod, watching him quizzically while she treaded water a short distance away. The underwater pool lights faithfully outlined her, reminding him of what was so near and what he had no right to touch.

She moved closer, placing her hand beside his on the tile railing of the pool.

"Dane?"

"Hmmmm?"

"Are you upset about anything?"

He eyed her warily. "No, why?"

"I don't know. You just seem jumpy, as though something is bothering you. I thought a swim might help to relax you."

He lifted one brow slightly. "Oh, you did, did you? It had nothing to do with your wanting to swim, I take it. My, the sacrifices you're prepared to make in order to entertain out-of-town guests."

Her predictable temper got the better of her and she suddenly hit the water with both hands, causing a wave to break over him. Then she swam underwater toward the other end of the pool. Just as she came up for air, Dane was waiting for her. Giving her only enough time to get a mouthful of air, he pushed her back under.

No matter where she tried to go in the pool, he was waiting for her, until they were both panting from the exertion. At one point she managed to break free of him, only to have him grab her ankle and inexorably pull her back to him.

"Give up, tadpole. You can't win," he said between breaths.

They were in the middle of the pool. Dane was able to stand, but the water was over Felicia's head. He heard her labored breathing and, without considering the consequences, pulled her into his arms.

He should have known that she'd never admit defeat. She would have drowned first. With his arm around her waist he swam for the side.

She hung on to him limply, her head docilely resting on his shoulder, while she worked to get her breath.

"I didn't intend to drown you, you know," he murmured, holding her close. The buoyancy of the water floated her closer to him. Her legs entangled with his until he realized she was straddling his thigh. Her thin panties seemed to be nonexistent as he felt the warmth of her. Her thighs clamped around him in an unconscious invitation.

Dane glanced down at her as Felicia slowly raised her head from his shoulders. Water still clung to her long lashes, making them heavy and giving her a sleepy, seductive look. Their breathing had returned to normal—almost.

Succumbing to the overwhelming temptation, Dane placed his lips on hers in a soft kiss. They felt cool and moist. Her mouth opened beneath his—so naturally, so inevitably, that he let go of the side of the pool to pull her even closer. The water provided a warm cocoon of sensation as her body glided smoothly against him.

It was only when Dane realized he couldn't breathe that he kicked them back to the surface. This time he found his footing in shallower water.

Once again they were both gasping for air, but when their lungs filled this time their mouths blindly searched for each other again. Dane felt as though he were on fire, and half expected the water to start boiling around him. The slight lapping of the water around his shoulders teased his senses, until he felt as though he were drowning in a sea of sensual sensation.

Dane forced himself to raise his head and looked down into Felicia's upturned face. Her eyes were closed, her lips slightly swollen from the pressure of his kisses. He could feel her breasts against his chest while she took quick, shallow breaths.

Never before had Dane come so close to losing complete control of himself.

"Felicia?" he whispered.

"Mmmmm?" She didn't open her eyes.

"I think we've done enough swimming for one evening, don't you?"

"Oh, yes," she agreed emphatically without opening her eyes. She continued to hang on to him as he moved toward the steps in the shallow end of the pool.

Dane slipped his arms under her thighs and shoulders. Once out of the pool, he lowered her legs and reached for the towel she had left on a chair.

Carefully stepping back from her, he wrapped the towel around her. Grabbing his Levi's he tossed them across his shoulder and walked Felicia back to the room, his arm around her shoulders.

The air felt cool on his wet skin and Dane forced himself to concentrate on the night around them, on anything except the woman walking close beside him.

Once inside the room he refused to look at her. Instead he searched his bag, found a shirt and handed it to her.

"Get out of those wet clothes and put this on. Then I'll drive you back to the dorm."

Felicia disappeared into the bathroom without a word. As soon as the door closed, Dane grabbed a towel and hurriedly began to dry off. After he changed into a dry pair of briefs he pulled on his Levi's, feeling the dampness where they had rested against his wet skin.

He was towel-drying his hair when he heard the bathroom door open. He tensed at the sound, then glanced around. His shirt hung to her knees. The lightweight material could not conceal that she no longer wore a bra. He was also aware that, if she'd followed his directions, she no longer wore panties, either.

How had he allowed himself to get into this situation?

"Are you ready to go?" he asked gruffly.

Felicia's eyes glowed. Her skin shone with a satiny gleam, and he tried to ignore how she looked, standing there in front of him.

"No. I don't want to go. I want to stay with you." Her smile made his heart pause in its rapid beat. She placed her palms on his bare chest, leaning lightly into him. Dane knew at that moment that he had lost the battle—with her, with himself and with his conscience. Blindly he reached for her, wrapping his arms around her and pulling her tightly against his aroused body.

Three

The rhythmic swish of the wipers provided a steady undertone for the sound of the hard driving rain. The varied noises slowly found their way into Felicia's consciousness. Forcing her eyes open, she realized that night had fallen. She straightened slightly and glanced at the man sitting beside her, gripping the wheel, his expression remote and forbidding. Whatever his thoughts, they weren't pleasant.

"Where are we?" she asked, trying to peer through the rain and gloom for familiar landmarks.

"About a mile out of Mason," he responded.

"Why are we going into Mason?" The county road leading to the ranch was at least ten miles east of the county seat on the Fredericksburg Highway.

"I thought we'd stop and eat before going home. I wasn't sure when we'd get back, so I told Millie not to bother fixing anything for us."

With her mind on Adam and his disappearance, Felicia hadn't given a thought to Millie, which was unforgivable. Millie had been an institution in her life since her mother had died.

"How is Millie?"

"Same as usual."

"Hasn't thrown up her hands in disgust trying to look after two crusty old bachelors, huh?" Her light tone gave out midway through the sentence, breaking into a husky whisper.

"He's okay, Felicia. Who knows? He may already be at the ranch by the time we get there."

"You don't really believe that, do you?"

He was silent, watching the road. Just before they reached the bridge outside of Mason he turned to the left onto a road that led to more ranchland.

"Where are we going to find a place out here to eat?" she asked, bewildered.

"I thought we'd eat at The Homestead. It's a restaurant built on one of the old places. I think you'll like it."

They drove up a lane that didn't seem to be marked with any signs, through a gate standing hospitably open, and she saw what must be the restaurant. It looked just like what Dane had called it, a homestead, with warm light shining from several windows. Two rooms built in the traditional log-cabin style were well lit, inviting hungry visitors inside. As soon as Dane opened the door for her, Felicia caught the scent of wood burning and saw a massive fireplace at one end of the room, the fire dancing and snapping merrily. A half-dozen people were seated at small tables around the room.

A blond woman with a cheerful smile and dancing eyes greeted them. "Well, hello, Dane. I didn't expect we'd see you out on a night like this." She led them over to one of the small tables in front of the fireplace, placing handmade menus in front of them. Felicia felt the warmth and friendliness radiating from both the fire and the lady who stood there, smiling.

"Charlotte, I want you to meet Adam's sister. This is Felicia St. Clair." He glanced over at Felicia. "Charlotte is the owner of The Homestead."

If anything, Charlotte's smile grew broader. "I'm so pleased to meet you, Felicia. I've heard so much about you from Dane and Adam I feel like I know you."

She could hear the affection in Charlotte's voice when she mentioned the men's names. They obviously knew one another well.

Charlotte took their orders and disappeared in the kitchen. Felicia looked around the room, taking in the deep-set windows, the tiled floor, the heavy beamed ceiling, and smiled. "They found a good name for the place, didn't they?"

"After we eat I'll show you the other side. Although they built this room to match, the other side is an authentic, pioneer log cabin. They bought it, dismantled it, moved it to this location and reassembled it. They even have the loft intact, where some of the original family must have slept."

"I'm glad you brought me here," she managed to say. "Thank you."

In the car she could pretend she wasn't with Dane, had even managed to sleep for a while in order to shorten the time they had to talk. But in the soft lamplight of the restaurant she was forced to look at what her heart had never forgotten.

If possible, Dane had grown more handsome since she'd seen him last. At thirty-seven, his thick, black hair was beginning to show flecks of silver around his ears. It was still hard for her to believe that he had remained single. Any eligible woman in the vicinity of Mason County could scarcely be unaware of his attractiveness.

Perhaps he preferred to play the field. The only thing she knew for sure was that he didn't want her. He'd made that extremely clear five years ago and she would do well to remember that. She wasn't looking forward to spending any time around him, but at least she had managed to develop some pride. She never intended for him to know how much he had hurt her.

He was her brother's partner. That's all he was. That's all he would ever be. His rejection of her had left permanent scars on her heart. He would never get a chance to hurt her again.

"I intend to go to Monterrey," she said after Charlotte had served their meal and left the room once more.

Dane's head jerked up. "The hell you are. Why?"

She had known he wouldn't approve, but Felicia had long since given up trying to gain Dane's approval. "To find Adam."

"You've got to be out of your mind. Authorities from two countries have been searching. What makes you think you can do any better?"

"I don't. I just know that I can't sit by and wait. I have to do something."

"It's too dangerous," he stated in a flat tone.

"People go down there all the time. There's nothing dangerous about it."

"Even though Adam might argue the point?" he asked grimly.

She didn't need to be reminded. Perhaps it was dangerous, but that wasn't going to deter her. She continued to eat, determined not to let him upset her.

"What do you think?" Dane asked a few minutes later.

"About what?"

He motioned to her plate. "The food."

"Oh! It's marvelous. They have a great cook."

"Yes. Charlotte's daughter."

"She doesn't look old enough to have a grown daughter."

Dane grinned. "You should tell her that. It would make her day."

Felicia was aware of how easily Dane fell into the familiar banter they had shared when she'd lived at home. He seemed so relaxed around her, but, then, why shouldn't he be? His feelings had never been involved. She'd just been too young to understand that a man can be physically aroused by a woman without loving her or wanting a permanent relationship.

If nothing else, she'd learned that lesson well while living in L.A. Her friends couldn't understand why she didn't date. She had tried and was appalled by the upwardly mobile young men who expected instant gratification from the woman they deigned to invite to dinner.

She hadn't known how to deal with them without feeling foolish, so she stopped accepting invitations.

Felicia felt sure Dane never lacked for feminine companionship.

The rain had slackened some by the time they left, but the wind was cold. Los Angeles had caused Felicia to forget what a cold winter could feel like. At least it hadn't gotten cold enough to snow.

"You aren't serious about going to Mexico, are you?" Dane asked once they pulled up in front of the house. He turned in the seat, his arm sliding along the back so that his hand was almost touching her shoulder.

"Yes. I'm very serious."

"What about your job?"

"What about it?"

"How much time will they allow you to take off?"

"I explained that it was a family emergency and that I would be in touch. My assistant can handle the routine things. If not, she's to call me."

"But how will she find you if you're off beating the bushes in Mexico?"

"Why don't you let me worry about that? Why all this sudden concern about my career, Dane?"

"It isn't sudden. I've always been interested in your career."

"Of course you have."

"Whatever happened to your plans to become a writer?"

"I am a writer."

"Then I should say a rich and famous one?"

"I enjoy what I do and I make all the money I need. I get enough recognition of my skills to be content."

"Quite a change."

"Not really. I got over most of those silly dreams before I ever left high school."

"You never bothered to tell Adam," he pointed out thoughtfully.

"Oh, he never paid any attention to my fantasies."

"Don't be so sure. He talked about you often, you know. He was so proud that you finished college, when he didn't. That you had the dreams and ambition to go on with a career, when he was content to come back and manage the ranch."

He got out of the car and came around to open her door, but she was already out of the car and heading toward the porch. He stood there for a moment and watched her straight back as she climbed the steps, fiercely independent.

Regardless of what she said, he knew she would never have been content to settle down and become a rancher's wife. Just as he knew that he would never be happy living anywhere else but a ranch.

He walked back around the car and got in, pulling it into the multicar garage, where it would be out of the weather.

Dane walked into the house. There was a note on the kitchen table listing the calls that had come in for him while he was gone.

There was no word about Adam.

Dane straightened slowly, running his hand through his hair. He'd had a rough two days— what with the news about Adam, having to contact Felicia and now, having her home again.

He wished to hell he knew how to keep her out of Mexico. He knew better than to try to use threats. Once she got the bit between her teeth, there was no controlling her. He knew that as well as anyone.

Dane crossed the hall to the living room to turn off the lamp Millie had left on for them and was surprised to find Felicia standing in the middle of the room. He had thought she'd gone on upstairs to bed.

She turned when she heard his step, and he saw tears in her eyes.

"It all looks so familiar," she said with a catch in her voice.

"I know."

"I don't know why I expected it to change." She pointed to the draperies. "I had those made up to match the sofa and chairs just before I left. I remember Adam teasing me about making the place look so fancy." She ran her hand over the books in the bookcase. "He saved all my books, even the textbooks."

Tears glistened as they ran down her cheeks. "It's just as though I left this morning. And Adam will come stomping in from the porch any minute now, tracking in mud and laughing about the weather."

He couldn't stand to see her pain. In two long strides Dane reached her side and pulled her roughly into his arms. She stiffened at his touch, but he didn't let go, and gradually he felt her relax against him. Dane buried his hands in her hair, holding her close.

God, she felt so good to him. How long had it been since he'd had her in his arms? Too long. How had he found the strength to let her go? The truth was, he'd had no choice.

She wanted no part of the only kind of life he could live. He'd known that about both of them from the time they'd first met. If only he could control the strong physical attraction that still existed between them.

Felicia gave up battling her tears and let them flow. She hadn't cried when she'd gotten the call about Adam. She wasn't sure of all the reasons she was crying now. Too many things had happened, too many memories had surfaced, and she'd had to face too many unpleasant truths.

She had missed her home. She hadn't allowed herself to realize how much until she had walked in tonight. Her parents' wedding picture still hung on the wall, as well as various snapshots of her and Adam and occasionally one of their mother, who preferred taking the pictures rather than being in them.

She'd missed Pete and Millie and her friends. She'd missed Blaze and riding him whenever she couldn't stand being cooped up in the house another minute.

And even though she talked with Adam frequently and saw him at least twice a year, she had to face how much she missed him. And loved him.

The most traumatic truth Felicia faced during the past few hours was how she felt about Dane Rineholt. He was so much a part of her past. There was no way she could ignore the years she had shared with him. She loved him. What she felt was no schoolgirl crush, unfortunately.

When he had first put his arms around her a few minutes ago she had thought she would cry out with the intensity of the emotion that swept over her.

His hands slowly stroked her back and he murmured quietly into her ear, ''He's going to be okay, love. He'll be home soon.''

If only she *were* his love. Dane had the ability to set off explosive sparks of feeling within her like no other man could do and Felicia realized that her arms had gone around his waist. She was hugging him with a fierce intensity.

Of course he was only trying to comfort her. She knew that. Felicia was no longer the naive young woman she had been the last time she had been in his arms. She would not misinterpret his actions this time.

Fighting for some control over her emotions, she loosened her hold around Dane's waist. As though reluctant to let her go, Dane slowly dropped his arms and stepped back from her.

With calm deliberation, Felicia met his gaze, forcing herself not to flinch at the unexpected warmth in his eyes.

"I intend to leave tomorrow."

"If you insist," he replied.

She was surprised that he didn't continue to try to talk her out of it. Dropping her eyes from his distracting gaze, she turned toward the stairs. "It's late. I'm going to bed." When he didn't say anything, she looked back at him and attempted to smile. "I'll see you tomorrow."

"Yes, you will," he agreed. "If you insist on going to Mexico, I'm going with you."

His tone of voice made it very clear that he had no intention of changing his mind.

Part of her reason for leaving so soon was to get away from Dane. So much for that idea. However, she hadn't looked forward to making the trip alone, either. Perhaps Dane was right. She didn't have any of the details surrounding Adam's disappearance. There could very well be danger involved in a search. Despite the pain of being around him, Felicia knew there was no one she'd rather have on her side if the going got rough.

Nodding in acceptance, Felicia went upstairs to the room that had been hers for twenty-seven years. It looked the same, as though she'd never left it. Of course Millie must have known she was coming. The furniture gleamed in the soft lamplight and Felicia ran her hand across the crazy quilt that had always been on her four-poster as a spread.

Her mother had made it, taking scraps of the clothes Felicia had outgrown and cutting them into patterns to be stitched into colorful squares. Her bedroom was a far cry from her modern apartment in L.A. More than miles separated the two. At issue was an entirely different life-style and thinking pattern.

Feeling totally drained, Felicia tossed back the covers and wearily crawled into bed.

Perhaps it was being home again that triggered old memories that helped form her dreams. Felicia found herself waking up with a start two or three times, memories of Adam and Dane bouncing around in her head.

In particular she kept recalling her senior year at the university, when she'd finally gotten up the nerve to invite Dane to escort her to one of the graduation dances.

Never had she been so surprised as she was when he'd accepted her invitation. And never more excited. Of course her friends had heard all about Dane Rineholt. Her roommate pointed out that she fully expected to find that he walked on water and teasingly asked her if he'd give them a demonstration.

Felicia didn't mind the kidding. She was in love with Dane Rineholt and didn't care who knew it—except Dane himself, of course. She still squirmed with embarrassment whenever she thought about the time she had told him she loved him. He hadn't believed her. He'd even mocked her, and his response had hurt.

During the four years Felicia was away at school, she had adopted a casually friendly attitude with Dane. She rarely saw him except for an occasional meal at home. For a while

Felicia fully expected to hear an announcement that he was getting married. He was seen with JoBeth Lawson for more than a year and speculation about a wedding was mentioned frequently by the townsfolk.

Felicia tried not to think about how she would handle the news that Dane Rineholt intended to marry someone else. During her years in college, she kept herself too busy to have much time to think about the possibility. She worked at the offices of the *Mason County News*, the small weekly paper published in her hometown, during her summer vacations, learning how to write the concise articles that were necessary in order to give the pertinent facts.

She also helped to sell advertising, the lifeblood of any newspaper, and gained a real appreciation for the hard work that went into such an effort.

If anyone had asked her that spring what her hopes and dreams were, she could have readily listed them. She wanted to marry Dane Rineholt, return to the ranch that had always been her home, help with the local paper and try her hand at writing a novel. Since Dane had not announced his engagement by her senior year, Felicia had begun to hope that he'd been waiting for her to finish school.

Now all she needed to do was to convince Dane she was old enough to settle down.

The question was, did he love her? And if he did, did he want to marry her?

It was no wonder she was nervous when she came downstairs at the dorm to meet him.

Dressed in jeans and a work shirt Dane Rineholt was definitely worth a second glance. In evening wear he took her breath away.

She began to relax with him as the evening progressed. He seemed amiable enough, chatting with her friends, taking their gentle teasing in good spirit. However, it was later, while they were swimming, that Felicia began to hope that all of her dreams were about to come true.

Dane didn't kiss her as though he still saw her as a child. And there was no way he could hide from her his physical reaction to their closeness.

She couldn't control the shiver of anticipation that ran through her when she walked out of the bathroom and found Dane standing there, wearing only a pair of jeans. His broad shoulders were tanned from the sun, the muscles rippling as he towel-dried his hair.

When he looked at her he slowly lowered his arms, and the towel dropped, unheeded, to the floor. The look in his eyes was one she had seen several times that evening. It was a look that she found extremely encouraging. Whatever else Dane was thinking, she knew he was not indifferent to her.

When his arms wrapped around her, she knew she was where she wanted to be. It didn't matter to her that he hadn't told her he loved her. She could tell from his lean, hard body that he wanted her. And she wanted him. So very much.

His mouth came down on hers in a desperate possession, one that she was willing to allow. How many years had she dreamed of this moment with this man?

His kiss was even better than she remembered. She loved the feel of him so close to her and she felt her knees give way. Without taking his mouth from hers, he scooped her up in his arms and carried her to the nearby bed.

Both of them fell across the bed, their arms entwined, their mouths still touching. The shirt she wore had ridden up on her hip and his hand found her bare skin and gently rubbed across it, back and forth, until she thought she would cry out with the intensity of the feeling his touch aroused within her.

She couldn't resist touching his chest, something she had often yearned to do. Her sensitive fingertips found the flat nipples half-hidden in his curling chest hair and she felt them harden.

His hand shifted slightly, and as he ran his hand softly from the top of her rib cage to where her thighs met her stomach muscles involuntarily tightened at the unfamiliar sensation.

Felicia pulled back slightly, trying to get her breath. She gazed into his blazing eyes and reminded herself to relax. This was Dane and anything he did was all right.

With probing fingers he caressed her, touching her with gentle tenderness. She found that she wanted to touch him, and she slid her hand into his jeans, feeling the hardness there—a smooth hardness that she found deliciously fascinating.

Dane lowered his head and nudged the shirt aside with his mouth, and found the tip of her breast. His tongue gently caressed the point until the nipple grew taut. Then his lips slipped over the pebblelike hardness and coaxed it into his mouth.

Felicia thought she was going to explode with the intensity of her feelings. Tears ran unheeded down her cheeks.

Dane shifted on the bed, one leg thrown across her thighs as he gathered her closer.

One moment he was kissing her passionately, his tongue imitating the erotic rhythm of his fingers, the next moment he froze.

Pulling away slightly, he looked down at her. Felicia opened her eyes and saw the slight flush on his cheeks, the tautness in his jaw and the hot gleam in his eyes.

"What's wrong?" she asked breathlessly.

With deliberation he moved his hand away from her thighs and glared at her accusingly.

"You're a virgin," he stated in a flat voice.

"Yes," she agreed, bewildered.

"I didn't realize."

"Does it matter?"

"Of course it matters." He sat up on the side of the bed.

"Why?"

"I thought you had some experience."

"And now that you know I don't?"

"I'm not the one who's going to give it to you."

"I don't understand."

"You came here tonight looking for fun and excitement."

"That's not true."

"Or maybe this is some sort of initiation rite you and your friends dreamed up."

"No!"

He ran his hand over his already mussed hair. "Well, whatever the reason, I don't intend to be a part of it."

"But you wanted me!"

He glanced over his shoulder at her, then reached over and pulled the shirt she wore down, covering her thighs.

"You're a very attractive woman," he admitted.

"But you don't love me, is that it?"

He lifted a brow slightly in an all-too-familiar expression of amused irony. "Love has nothing to do with what almost happened tonight."

Felicia felt a sharp pain in her chest, as though a doubled fist had hit her, knocking the breath from her lungs. "You really are a bastard, aren't you, Dane," she managed to say after a moment.

"Maybe I am, but I don't accept virginal offerings from young ladies eager to learn about life. You'll have to find someone else for that."

Felicia scrambled off the bed, wanting to get as far away from him as possible.

"I hate you."

"I'm sure you do. At the moment, anyway. Tell me, was this some sort of bet you made, to see if you could seduce me tonight?" When she refused to speak, he shrugged and drawled, "Well, for the record, you almost won. Another few minutes and I would have been unable to..."

"You don't need to lecture, Mr. High and Mighty Rineholt. You've made your point. I don't know why I ever thought I was in love with you. I must have been out of my tiny little mind to think I'd ever be happy married to an autocratic, dictatorial, arrogant—"

"Married!" Dane almost flinched when she said the word.

"Don't worry, Dane. I don't intend to blackmail you into marrying me, even though

Adam might be curious about my being here with you tonight."

"I did not invite you here, Felicia. If you want, you may tell Adam whatever suits you, so long as you keep your facts straight."

Felicia had never felt so humiliated in her life. The tender feelings she'd enjoyed only a short time ago had been lacerated beyond belief. For what reason? None of this scene made any sense to her.

Spinning around, she grabbed her dress and rushed into the bathroom. Jerking off his shirt, she once again put on the dress that earlier that evening she'd slipped on with such a keen sense of anticipation.

All her dreams had been shattered. Dane Rineholt didn't love her—never did and never would. The sooner she accepted that, the better.

When she returned to the bedroom she was once again in control of her emotions. She noticed with relief that Dane had dressed and was standing by the door, his car keys in hand. He opened the door without speaking and she walked out into the hallway.

They were in the car and on the way to the dorm, when Felicia spoke. "I don't intend to mention this to Adam," she said quietly.

"Neither do I."

"I feel so ashamed."

"Don't be. Neither one of us was thinking clearly tonight."

She could handle his cold aloofness better than the understanding she heard in his voice. A lump formed in her throat and she was afraid she was going to burst into tears. *Not now! Hang on until he's gone.*

She glanced over at him, his profile periodically highlighted as they passed under streetlights. It was time to quit living in her dreamworld and face reality. All she was, all she had ever been to Dane, was Adam's kid sister. He was willing to go to bed with her when he thought she had some experience. If not, he wasn't even interested in her at all.

"I wonder if you'll ever see me as an adult?" she asked, giving voice to her thoughts.

He pulled up in front of her dorm, got out, walked around the car and opened her door.

When she stood, he tilted her chin up with his forefinger.

"I hope not, tadpole. Because if and when I do, the good Lord have mercy on my soul." He leaned down and placed his cool, firm lips against hers for a brief moment, then pulled away. "Good night, Felicia."

She stood in the doorway and watched until the red taillights of his car blinked out of sight.

Dane Rineholt was not going to be a part of her life. She had no choice but to accept that fact.

At the moment she wasn't at all sure she could live without him, not if she had to see him every day.

With that thought in mind, Felicia began to plan for a future that did not include Dane.

The sound of a phone ringing repeatedly finally broke through Felicia's consciousness and she realized she'd been dreaming once again ... or reliving past memories. Whatever she called it, the story remained the same, never varying, no matter how much she hoped for a different outcome.

She sat up in bed and realized she was no longer in her apartment in California. Instead, the same dresser that she'd had as far back as she could remember faced the bed where she slept.

Groping for the switch on the lamp beside her bed, Felicia threw back the covers and stood up. By the time she found the lamp, the ringing had stopped. She looked at her watch. It was almost three o'clock in the morning.

She quietly opened her bedroom door and listened. Had someone answered it before whoever was calling gave up? Attempting to still the rapid rhythm of her heart, she tried to listen for any sound to break the silence of the house. Faintly she heard a voice.

Stepping out into the hallway, Felicia tiptoed toward the stairs. The voice was downstairs. It sounded like Dane.

As quietly as possible, Felicia went downstairs, then paused in the doorway of the office where Dane stood, clad only in a pair of jeans, listening on the phone. He had his back to her.

"She's insisting on going down there," she heard him say, and realized he was talking about her.

"You don't know this woman if you think I've got any influence over what she does," he continued.

Felicia felt guilty standing there listening when he didn't know she was there, but on the other hand, she was vitally interested in the conversation. Who was calling and what connection did the person have with Dane and Adam?

"I can't tell her anything. You know that. It's too dangerous."

A sudden spurt of adrenaline shot through her body at his words. Her instinctive sense that there was something about Adam's disappearance that didn't ring true sharpened. Felicia wouldn't have retreated from listening to that conversation if someone had suddenly pointed a gun to her head! Adam was in danger and Dane knew why!

"Thanks for the report," he was saying to whoever was on the line. "Yeah, I wish the news had been better myself." A long pause ensued. "I know. The only thing I can do is go with her and try to keep her out of trouble." Another pause. "Damn it, I know that! And if you think you can handle the situation any better, you're certainly welcome to try!"

Dane walked over to the massive fireplace and placed his forearm on the mantel above it. Wearily he rested his head on his arm while he listened.

"There's no help for it that I can see. I'll just play it by ear. Hopefully you'll find him before she gets too involved. Then it's up to him to decide what to tell her."

After another lengthy pause, he raised his head slowly. "I'll stay in touch for the latest developments. As soon as we get down there I'll check in and give you our location." He nodded in silent confirmation. "Talk to you later."

He turned to hang up the phone and saw Felicia standing inside the doorway. Without a change of expression, he placed the phone on the receiver and deliberately studied her, making her conscious for the first time that she had trotted downstairs wearing a very skimpy nightshirt.

For the first time she was aware of the chill of the hardwood floor against her bare toes, and she took a couple of steps into the room so that she could stand on the large area rug that gave warmth and color to the room.

"You're going to catch cold coming downstairs like that," he commented quietly. "I turn the furnace down at night."

She glanced at his chest, then down to his bare feet. "I could say the same about you."

He smiled slightly, but the smile never reached the watchful intensity of his eyes. "I know. We really should have an extension put in upstairs, but there never really seemed to be a need for one before. Our phone seldom rings after eight o'clock in the evening."

"Who called?"

He shrugged, crossing the room to where she stood. He placed his hand on her shoulder as though to turn her toward the door. "Just a business associate."

"Your business associate keeps some rather strange hours, don't you think?"

His chuckle seemed relaxed and unconcerned. "That's true enough." He frowned slightly when she resisted the pressure on her shoulder and held her ground.

"Who is he?"

He paused in front of her, his frown deepening. "No one you'd know."

"But he knows Adam."

"Of course," he said a trifle impatiently.

"Did he have anything to do with his disappearance?" she asked calmly.

He stared down at her in silence for a moment. "What's that supposed to mean?" he finally asked.

She crossed her arms, trying to hide the trembling that had overtaken her, partly from the slight chill of the room and partly because of nerves.

"I want to know what's going on."

Her statement hung between them like a sudden puff of smoke without enough moving air to dissipate it. She refused to drop her gaze, but determinedly met his.

He shook his head slightly. "You know as much as I do, Felicia."

"And that's a lie," she responded swiftly.

A muscle jumped in his cheek, the only sign that indicated he wasn't as relaxed as his stance in front of her would suggest. Slowly he loosened his grasp on her arm and allowed his hand to drop away.

"What do you want to know?" He never took his eyes off her and she absently rubbed her hands over her forearms in agitation.

"I want to know what Adam was doing in Mexico, who he went to see and why, and any ideas you have as to what might have caused his disappearance."

He rubbed the tight muscles in his neck with his hand while he continued to study her determined face. "I don't suppose we could postpone this discussion until morning, could we?'' he asked in a wistful tone. Her gaze never wavered, and after a minute or more of silence he said, ''I guess not.''

As though making a decision, he suddenly turned and walked into the hallway. ''All right, Felicia. I'll answer your questions. But I'll be damned if I'm going to stand there and shiver while I do it. I'm going up to put on a shirt and some shoes. I suggest you do the same. We might as well be comfortable.''

He disappeared from view and she heard his measured steps going up the stairway. It was all she could do to keep from screaming and throwing something. The man was always so controlled. What feelings he might possess never seemed to get in the way of how he behaved.

Felicia's thoughts returned to the night five years ago when he had almost made love to her. Almost, until he had decided it wasn't the thing to do. Ignoring his obvious physical reaction to her, he'd determined not to allow his emotions to rule his head.

Damn him. What sort of man was he to exert so much control over his emotions and actions? A small voice answered her, *obviously a man you want on your side and not against you.*

Recognizing that there was no need to stay downstairs and shiver, she decided to take his advice and get dressed.

By the time she'd returned, Dane had coffee made and a fire going in the den. He sat in one of the large overstuffed chairs in front of the fireplace, sipping from a large mug while gazing into the fire. He'd put on a heavy gray sweater that fit his shoulders as though it had been made for him. Since the color of the soft yarn exactly matched the color of his eyes, there was a good chance the sweater had been a gift that had indeed been knitted especially for him.

Felicia walked in and saw that he had brought the coffee and another cup from the kitchen. Picking up the glass carafe, she poured some of the brew into the cup and sat down in the matching chair in front of the fire.

"Do you think Adam is alive?" was her first question.

As though reluctant to leave the view of the flickering flames, Dane slowly lifted his eyes until his gaze met hers.

"I hope to God he is. If not, I'm responsible for his death."

There was so little expression in his voice that for a moment she missed the import of his words. When they registered, she almost flinched.

The lines in his face had deepened and for the first time since she had known him, Dane looked his age.

Felicia waited, knowing there was more, also knowing that he would tell her only what he chose, no matter how she begged or threatened. Now was the time to exert patience.

He almost smiled at the obvious struggle going on within her, and she resented his knowledge of her. Outside of Adam, this man knew her better than anyone. After all, he'd lived with her for years. How could he not know her moods, her foibles, her strengths and her weaknesses?

"Go on," she finally said when he leaned over and poured himself another cup of coffee.

"I've been working with a government covert operation for years—ever since I was in the service—on the drug problems that have plagued the United States. I became more ac-

tive about five years ago as the economic situation across the border became more acute
and drugs seemed to be pouring across the
river at an increased rate.'' He paused, taking
a sip of his coffee and staring once again at the
fire that had taken the chill off the room.

Without looking back at her, he continued.
''Because of my increased absences away from
the ranch I had to explain to Adam what I was
doing and why. I don't suppose anyone can
understand why a person would be willing to
get involved in tracking down drug smugglers
unless he's seen what drug addiction does to a
person. One of my brothers got involved with
them and almost died.

''Although he survived an overdose, Johnny
suffered considerable damage. He'll never be
the same again. I made a promise to myself
when I stood over him in that hospital bed that
I was going to do everything in my power to
stop the people who were bringing this poison
into our lives.''

Felicia could feel his pain and knew that
whatever else Dane was, he loved his family,
and she hurt for him, beginning to recognize
the helpless feeling of wanting to help a loved
one but not knowing how.

"Our group is always understaffed, and when Adam offered to help I wasn't firm enough in my refusal to have him involved. He understood my feelings. Pointed out it could have been him as much as Johnny. In the end, he outtalked me." He glanced back at her. "That was four years ago."

"So you think his disappearance is drug related?"

"There's a strong possibility. The longer we go without word from him, the less likely are his chances of being found alive."

Felicia could feel the cold fist of fear tightening in her chest. It had never completely left her since the night she'd received Dane's call telling her of Adam's disappearance.

"Do you know who he was going to see?"

"No. He was following up some leads of his own. We tended to work independently of each other, which has worked to our benefit in the past. He had several contacts down there I knew nothing about. But he'd given his superior some needed information just before he went down there, enough to give the authorities a couple of leads to follow. That call tonight was to let me know the leads so far had turned up nothing."

Felicia stared blindly into the fireplace. Not Adam, dear God. Please. Not Adam. She could see his laughing face, his eyes full of mischief, hear his teasing tone. And he was so young. He'd be thirty-two next month. He'd had a man's responsibility most of his life—for his mother and sister and the ranch. And for the past fifteen years he'd played both mother and father to her.

Adam had always taken his responsibilities seriously, so he wouldn't have shirked helping Dane, understanding why Dane was involved.

"I've got to know," she murmured, her voice barely audible.

"Believe me, I can understand your feelings. We'll be the first they notify when anything turns up."

She looked over at Dane. "You don't understand. I can't just sit here and wait. I want to be doing something. Anything."

Dane leaned forward in his chair, his elbows resting on his knees, his hands loosely clasped. "You think I don't understand? Don't you have any idea what it's doing to me sitting here, waiting for the phone to ring?"

"I'm still going down there," she stated firmly.

The corner of his mouth tilted up slightly. "Now why doesn't that come as a surprise to me?"

"I mean it."

"I know you do. I've seen that look on your face more than once."

"I'll put ads in the local paper, offering a reward. I'll talk to every employee of the hotel. I'll make such a stir that somebody somewhere is bound to notice."

"That's exactly what I'm afraid of."

"Nobody would dare harm me."

"Honey, that's the most dangerous fallacy of all." He stood and stretched his arms high above his head. "The type of people who deal in drugs have absolutely no compunction about snuffing out the lives of other people. None whatsoever. Their only motivation is greed. They do what they have to do to survive. Don't kid yourself that your life means anything to anyone involved down there."

She stood, too, facing him. "I don't care about the danger," she stated in a quiet voice. "All I care about is finding Adam."

"I know. And I'm going with you."

"You don't have to."

"Yes, I do. You and Adam are family. I'm not going to let you go alone." He shrugged. "Adam would never forgive me for allowing you to go down there on your own. They've never heard of women's rights down there, you know."

"I didn't think many men in Texas had, either, for that matter."

He grinned. "Oh, I don't know. We're getting downright civilized around here, little lady. Maybe if you stick around long enough, you'll find that out."

Perhaps it was because he smiled so seldom that Felicia found him so devastating. Whatever it was, the long years of absence seemed to have disappeared and she felt as shaky as the young woman who had gone with him to his motel room.

He would always have the power to make her tremble at his nearness. But at twenty-seven, she now knew how to disguise her reaction to him. Firmly she reminded herself that he saw her only as an extension of his own family. She wasn't going to embarrass either of them by asking for more.

"I suppose we'd better get some sleep," she said. "It will be light soon."

He nodded. "We'll make plans later this morning."

She smiled, a weary, touching smile that almost made Dane lose the control he'd managed to maintain during the past hour. He had wanted to hold and comfort her, protect her from what he and Adam had been doing, love her until her head was spinning. Instead he'd played the role he had adopted years ago—that of a member of the family.

He had to put out of his mind how Felicia had looked standing there in the doorway in her nightie that barely came down to her thighs. She had only grown more beautiful during the past few years.

And now he had to face the fact that starting later in the day they would be traveling together, staying together, working together. All the self-discipline that he'd gathered over the years was going to be called on during the next several days.

He could only pray that Adam would call shortly to say he was safe, so that Felicia could return to her other life and let him get on with his, with only the added memories of her visit home to keep him company.

Four

Felicia's sleep had been filled with dreams of Adam and Dane, of unknown, menacing threats, of voices speaking in a language she didn't understand. When a hand reached out and touched her shoulder, she screamed, throwing her body away from the predator, scrambling to get out from under entangling covers.

"I'm sorry, Felicia," Dane said. "I didn't mean to startle you."

At the first sound of his voice her eyes flew open, and she realized where she was. Feeling like a complete fool, she sat up in bed, distractedly shoving her hair away from her face.

"I was dreaming. I guess you fit into whatever was happening."

"I probably should have told her you'd call her back."

She glanced up at him. "Who? What are you talking about?"

"Jennifer is on the phone and asked to speak to you. Shall I tell her you'll call her later?"

She pushed the covers off and crawled out of bed. "No, I'll take it." There was no reason to be modest in front of Dane at this point, since she'd stood downstairs in front of him last night wearing the same gown. As nonchalantly as possible she picked up her warm robe and slipped her arms into it. She felt around for her slippers with her toes, found them and hastily slipped her feet into them.

Belting the robe as she went down the stairs, she thought about Jennifer. They had met when Felicia first went to work for the local paper, and had become good friends. Felicia had no idea how long Jennifer had worked there. All she knew was that Jennifer had taught her almost as much about journalism as she had learned at school, and imparted a great deal of practical knowledge that she had never acquired elsewhere.

"Good morning," she said into the phone.

"Felicia, I'm sorry to be bothering you your first day home, but I was so excited to hear you were in town I couldn't wait any longer to call."

"How did you know I was back?"

"Well, Roger said something about it. Said Emma was talking to someone who had seen you out at The Homestead last night. You know what small towns are like."

Indeed she did. A small town was like a large family. Everyone was interested in everyone else, and wanted to help a friend or neighbor who was ill or in trouble. And everyone had advice for everyone else.

She had almost forgotten. No one in her hometown would be able to understand that Felicia lived in an apartment complex where she didn't even know her neighbor's first name. The only reason she knew the last one was that it was on the mailbox.

"I wondered if you were free for lunch," Jennifer went on to say.

"Oh, Jennifer, I'm afraid not. I'm leaving today to visit with some friends farther south. But I'll be back here before I return to California. We'll get together then, okay?"

"That'll be fine. Adam is going to be so disappointed he missed you. He spends a great deal of his time these days traveling, you know."

"I know. But he enjoys it. That's the main thing." She could feel her nerves tightening at the thought that this was one trip he wasn't enjoying.

"Well, I won't keep you, then. Take care, and I'll see you when you get back. I can hardly wait to hear about your newest promotion on the magazine."

"Thanks for calling, Jennifer. I really appreciate your thinking of me."

"Oh, a day doesn't go by that I don't think of you out there in California, a big-time editor. You've really done well. Sometimes I can't help envying you the opportunity."

"Don't kid me, Jennifer. Nothing would pry you away from Mason, and you know it."

Jennifer laughed. "Maybe so. We'll never know, will we? Take care now."

Felicia slowly placed the receiver back on the phone. Jennifer's lilting voice had brought back so many memories of the good times she'd had growing up, her job working on the paper, and intermixed with all of those memories were those of Dane.

She'd had such a colossal crush on him. If only what she felt for him now could be so easily disposed of.

Dane placed a cup in her hand while she stood at the desk, staring unseeingly out the window.

"Millie has your breakfast ready."

She glanced down at the cup in her hand, then up at Dane. "Thank you."

"You're welcome," he responded, mimicking her polite voice.

She glanced at the clock that hung over the fireplace. Made from a slab of cedar that had been sanded and shellacked, it had hung there for more years than she could remember. Both hands pointed at eleven.

"Why didn't you wake me earlier?"

"I could see no reason to. You were obviously tired or you wouldn't have slept that long."

She reminded herself that her body was still functioning on Pacific Standard Time. It was only nine o'clock in California. Nevertheless she was used to getting up by six every day. *But you aren't used to getting up in the middle of the night to listen to phone conversations and discuss your brother's disappearance, either.*

"It's a good thing Jennifer called, then. I may have slept all day."

"Somehow I doubt it." As though unaware of the relaxed intimacy of the action, Dane rubbed her neck and shoulder muscles. Felicia wasn't aware of how tense she was until his large hands and strong fingers began to knead the flesh around her nape.

She dropped her chin a little, giving him access to her neck, and he continued to massage the area in long, gentle strokes.

"You'd better go eat," he said after a few minutes.

She nodded, refusing to look at him. Carefully carrying her coffee, she walked down the hallway to the kitchen.

"Good morning, Millie," she said cheerfully.

The short woman standing in front of the sink whirled around. "Felicia! My goodness, but it's wonderful to see you." She hastily dried her hands and hugged the taller woman. "What's taken you so long to come back home?"

"Oh, you know how it is. I was trying to get established in a new job, a new area." *Trying to make peace with my heart.*

"Come on in here and eat. We have a lot of catching up to do."

Millie sat down with a cup of coffee and proceeded to bombard Felicia with questions while she ate. Felicia noted that Dane hadn't followed her into the kitchen. Once in a while she could faintly hear him talking, so he must have been on the phone.

She wondered if he was making arrangements for them to travel south. She'd know soon enough. In the meantime she tried to answer Millie's questions, forcing herself to eat everything that had been prepared for her. She needed to keep up her strength.

"Dane tells me you two are leaving for Mexico today."

"Yes."

"I know you're worried about Adam."

"Yes."

"But gettin' yourself into a bunch of trouble down there isn't going to help Adam any."

"We won't get into any trouble."

"How can you be so sure? I doubt Adam expected any trouble, but it looks like he found plenty."

Millie's round face reflected her concern, and Felicia wished she knew how to reassure her. There was really nothing she could say.

Finishing her coffee, she stood. "That was delicious, Millie. Thank you." She leaned over and kissed the older woman on the cheek. "It's good to be home and have some of your cooking again."

"Nobody ever told you you had to leave," she mumbled, watching Felicia leave the room.

Felicia found Dane in the den, seated behind the desk, writing something. He looked up when she came through the doorway. "Finished?"

"Yes. I ate too much. But, then, I usually do when Millie's cooking. I don't know how you and Adam have managed to stay so slim all these years with her around."

Dane smiled. "We burn it off as soon as we eat it. You know that."

Yes. She'd seen the life that kept them hard as rock, lean and sinewy. She thought of the men she knew in California who lifted weights, jogged and ran in order to keep in condition. There wasn't one she could think of who could have worked next to either Dane or Adam without falling by the wayside. The hours at the ranch were long, the pay sometimes nonexistent, and she often wondered at the personality of men who were attracted to ranch life. They must need their freedom more than anything else to be willing to spend their lives ranching.

"Are you sure you want to leave today?"

Felicia braced herself for another argument. "Very sure. Why?"

"Because there's a long drive ahead of us, and I don't much care for driving through those mountains in Mexico after dark."

Felicia realized with some surprise and a great deal of pleasure that he was no longer fighting the issue of the proposed trip. He was pointing out the problems they would be facing and consulting her before making any decisions. He had accepted her as an equal, something he had never done before. Felicia was touched.

Dane waited for her response, recognizing with a wry self-knowledge that if she really wanted to begin their trip now, despite the weather and the long drive ahead of them, he would go along with her plan. If she but knew—there was nothing he wouldn't do for her. He'd faced that many years ago.

"Perhaps we could spend the night at the border and cross over into Mexico in the morning. Where were you planning to cross?"

"Laredo."

"We'd be well on our way into the mountains by midmorning if we stayed in Laredo tonight, don't you think?" she asked, studying the atlas he had spread out on the desk.

Dane glanced at her robe and slippers and asked, "Do you intend to travel dressed like that?"

She straightened and turned around. "I'm afraid this is a little too casual for traveling." She started for the door. "I should be ready to go in about twenty minutes," she added, heading for the stairs.

Dane stood there for a moment, a little surprised that she had taken his teasing so well. He almost missed the irate responses he used to get. Felicia had changed in many ways.

Looking out the window, he studied the sky. The wet norther that had blown in yesterday had left the Texas skies dark and cloudy. The rain had stopped, but the wind was cold and blustery and he didn't look forward to the drive south.

Part of the reason was that he didn't know what they would find. He wished to hell Felicia would change her mind about the trip. She had no idea what they were dealing with and he saw no point in going into graphic detail about what these people did to those they felt had betrayed them.

He hoped she never had reason to find out.

Dane heard Felicia coming down the stairs, and went out to meet her. She wore woolen slacks and a bulky turtleneck that brought out the color of her eyes, as though he needed reminding. Those eyes had haunted him for years. She looked sophisticated and elegant, not like the long-legged young girl who'd worn jeans and plaid shirts around the place. He doubted she even owned a pair of jeans anymore, unless they had some famous name stitched on the back pocket.

He took her bag out of her hand, then placed his other hand at the small of her back. "Where's your jacket?"

"Over there on the coat rack, next to yours."

He put the bag down and helped her with her jacket. Then, shrugging into his own, he picked up the bag once more.

Stepping outside, they were hit by a strong gust of wind as it swept around the corner of the house. Felicia staggered under the impact. Dane pulled her into the shelter of his arms, using his body to block as much of the wind as possible from her.

Felicia had trouble keeping up with his long strides as they crossed the ranch yard, but she appreciated his protection. She was breathless by the time she settled into the seat next to him, and she tried to convince herself the weather was to blame, and not being held so closely by Dane.

Their trip together was going to be every bit as uncomfortable as she had feared.

Felicia noticed that Dane seemed to be in a better mood today than when he'd first met her plane. Perhaps he had dreaded their meeting as much as she had. Felicia had no way of knowing. Dane had the most annoying habit of being impossible to read.

He and Adam were nothing alike. Yet over the years they had become close friends. She wondered if he'd ever opened up to Adam and talked. If he had, Adam would have never betrayed his confidence.

Thinking of Adam brought the whole scary nightmare back to her, and she shivered.

"Are you cold?"

Felicia looked around at Dane in surprise. "No, why?"

"I saw you shiver."

"Oh. No, I was thinking about Adam."

"I know this is hard on you, Felicia. We're doing everything we can at the moment. Try not to let your imagination run away with you."

"You're right, of course. But it's hard not to think about him. After all, that's why I'm here."

There was a moment of silence. "Oh, I've never had any doubt about that," he said dryly.

She looked at him, surprised at his tone.

He glanced over at her, then back at the road. "You made it clear you were kicking the

Texas dust from your feet five years ago when you left."

"Is that what you thought?"

"That's what Adam and I both thought. You certainly didn't prove us wrong, did you?"

"I had my reasons."

"I'm sure you did."

"I had something I had to prove—to myself and to you and Adam."

"Oh? What was that?"

"That I could make it on my own."

His soft laugh sounded relaxed and easy. "Honey, there was never a doubt in either one of our minds that whatever you went after, you'd get."

"Not everything," she murmured.

A reminiscent smile appeared on his face. "You were quite a handful back then. I'm surprised that Adam and I don't have more gray hair than we do."

"You never seemed to have any trouble dealing with me."

"You think not? I distinctly remember a few times that you definitely got the best of me." He shook his head. "There was one time in particular that I found myself way over my head before I knew what hit me."

"When was that?"

He glanced at her from the corner of his eye. "Oh, a few years ago. I doubt you'd even remember."

"Try me."

"The night I was foolish enough to take you back to my motel room in Austin—the year you graduated from college."

How could he possibly think she'd forget that night?

"You would have to bring up the most embarrassing evening of my life," she muttered. *And the most heartbreaking,* she silently added.

"Embarrassing?" he repeated thoughtfully. "I suppose it could have been for you."

"Yes. You made your position quite clear that night. You didn't intend to waste your time on an inexperienced woman."

"You couldn't be more wrong," he responded quietly.

Felicia realized that since he'd brought up the subject of that night in Austin her muscles had tightened, until she felt stiff. Forcing herself to relax, she tried to tell herself that nothing that happened that night made any difference to who she was today, but she knew better. What had happened, or hadn't happened, had had a profound effect on her and her feelings about herself and her ability to attract a man.

When she didn't say anything more, Dane spoke. "I don't believe you have any idea what being with you that night did to me. I was damned upset at myself because of my behavior. Over the years I had been rather proud of myself, the way I maintained my self-control around you. Yet it only took a few minutes during a midnight swim to destroy my illusions about myself." He glanced at her, but she didn't look at him. "I wanted to make love to you that night more than I've ever wanted anything in my life."

His quiet statement sent an electrical jolt through Felicia. There was no doubting the sincerity of his words, or the gruffness in his voice. She could almost feel the tension as it began to mount between them. "Then why didn't you?"

"Because one of us needed to hang on to his sanity. I figured that because I'm older, it had to be me. Making love to you would have complicated a situation that was already complicated enough.''

''But you were willing enough at first, until you discovered I'd never been with a man before.''

He remembered that moment as though it had just happened. He could almost feel her body pressed against him, taste the warmth of her mouth, see the satiny sheen of her skin in the soft lamplight. And he felt the shock all over again when he realized what he had been about to do.

''Discovering that was enough to bring me to my senses, thank God. I needed something to remind me that seducing you would end up in making both of us miserable.''

''How do you figure that?''

''You and I couldn't be more different if we tried, Felicia. We want different things from life. For years you made it plain that you were counting the days until you finished school and took off on a carefully planned career. That career didn't include life on a ranch.''

''It could have. Remember, I was raised on a ranch.''

''I know. And you hated it.''

''Where did you ever get that idea?''

"From Adam."

"Oh." She was quiet for several moments, looking back over the years from her adult perspective. She began to remember some of the conversations she and Adam had had before Dane appeared in their lives.

"There was a time when we weren't at all sure we'd be able to save the ranch," Felicia said thoughtfully. "Adam was so worried about what it would do to me to lose the only home I had known. Many of my remarks were made to reassure Adam that my world wouldn't come to an end if we lost the ranch. Then you came along." She stopped speaking, as though finished with her explanations.

"And?" he prompted when she remained silent.

"And—our lives changed. We didn't have to struggle so much. And I grew up."

"And fulfilled all your dreams and plans."

"Yes, I suppose."

"If I'd made love to you that night, we would have been married the next week. There would have been no job in L.A. No chance to spread your wings. Instead you'd still be living at the ranch."

Remembering the devastation she'd felt that night, Felicia wanted to scream at him that he hadn't understood at all, that nothing would have made her happier than to have married him five years ago. But, of course, it would do no good to admit that now. After waiting a few moments to ensure she had control of herself, Felicia said lightly, "Surely you don't expect me to believe you offer marriage to every woman you take to bed, Dane. If so, then I'm expected to believe a great number of women have turned you down over the years."

"I didn't say that. Besides, there haven't been all that many women." *Particularly after you came into my life,* he added silently. "You were different."

"I know. Inexperienced. Oh, well, that's all in the past now. Five years makes a difference." She was thinking about how her perspective had changed since that time. What she had assumed to be Dane's rejection of her had been a reflection of his sense of caring and responsibility. Dane had been strongly affected by the intimate circumstances. From her adult viewpoint, she recognized now that any man would have been affected. Dane hadn't been aware of how she felt about him and how much she wanted to be a part of his life. In his own way, Dane had been protecting her from herself and the choice she was trying to make.

From her new vantage point, she could better understand his concern. She couldn't help but wonder if things would have turned out differently if she'd been more open with him back then regarding her feelings. Would he have believed her and taken what she had so naively offered?

If he had, what would have happened to the career she had enjoyed these past few years? Felicia had no answers.

Dane felt a sharp, stabbing pain in the region of his heart at her words. *Five years makes a difference in experience.* He wondered why her comment should hit him so hard. He had always been aware of Felicia's passionate nature. She threw herself into everything she did with utmost abandon. Lovemaking would be the same way. She had been eager for him to show her that aspect of life. He had known at the time that once he made love to her, he'd never be able to let her go. No doubt she had found other men who weren't quite so primitively possessive.

He remembered how he had thought about her during the years she was in California, wondering what she was doing, who she was seeing and if she was falling in love. He kept waiting for her to come back and tell them she wasn't happy and that she wanted to return to Texas, but she never did. Instead she kept postponing her visits, as though she had more important things to do than to come home to Texas and to him.

His decision not to make love to her had been proven right. Too bad he didn't feel better about it. He'd spent many a long, lonely night imagining what would have happened if he hadn't stopped when he did, how she would have responded, how it would have felt to finally possess her.

There had been a time a couple of years ago when he'd come close to flying out to see her, to confront her with his feelings. But he hadn't.

Now she was back and they were being thrown into a situation of intimacy that he wasn't sure he could handle. He'd tried to treat her as he always had, and that might have worked if he could have kept a certain amount of distance between them. But sharing the car with her, having her nearby so that he caught the scent of her perfume, so close that he could touch her, played havoc with all his good intentions.

They drove for several miles, lost in their own thoughts, comparing the past to the present and wondering about the future.

"Are you hungry?" Dane finally asked.

"I could probably eat something. Why?"

"I didn't know if you wanted to stop and eat now or wait until we got to Laredo."

"How far are we?"

"We should be there in another hour."

"Why don't we wait? I think I'd prefer to have a shower and a nice, leisurely meal, maybe with a couple of glasses of wine, and just relax. How about you?"

Felicia acknowledged to herself that she was glad Dane had brought up that night five years ago. Facing the past had helped her make peace with herself and what had occurred then. The pain had disappeared, along with the sense of rejection she'd carried for years. She felt as though a tremendous weight had been removed from her. The burdens of the past shifted and disappeared, and for the first time in many years Felicia felt at peace.

Dane, on the other hand, had recognized that because his love for Felicia had not diminished at all over the years, being with her for the next few days was going to be a form of torture he would have preferred to avoid, if at all possible.

It wasn't possible. He wasn't going to let her go into Mexico alone. He would just have to make the best of the situation.

"Fine," he muttered after a lengthy pause.

Felicia looked at him in concern. His expression looked grim. She decided the strain of the past few days was showing on both of them. At least the rain had stopped, which should help the driving conditions somewhat. Rain squalls had been moving over them all afternoon. She was glad they weren't going into the mountains tonight.

Perhaps Dane would be able to relax over dinner.

They found a vacancy at a large motel in Laredo and checked into their rooms. They were located on the same floor and down the hall from each other. After carrying her bag into her room, Dane told her he'd return in half an hour.

He was as good as his word. When he tapped on the door Felicia was ready. She had changed into a long-sleeved dress that she felt would be warm enough without a jacket, since they were eating there in the motel.

Dane made no comment regarding her appearance, but not because he hadn't noticed. The slim-skirted dress hugged her slender body, subtly emphasizing the smooth line of her hips and waist. Its teal-blue color accented her eyes. Placing his hand lightly in the small of her back, Dane escorted her to the stairway. He was more than ready to have that drink she'd mentioned earlier.

Over dinner Felicia tried to draw him out. "The drive must have really been tiring for you," she offered with a sympathetic smile.

"Why do you say that?"

"You've been so quiet."

He took a swallow of the bourbon and water he'd ordered from the bar, then replied, "I've never been much for social conversation."

Felicia was surprised at his clipped tone. "You don't have to make social conversation with me, Dane. You know that. I was just concerned about you."

"Don't be." He watched her as she sat across from him, eating calmly. She seemed to take the ornate restaurant and modern motel in stride. "You've obviously gotten accustomed to motels," he said after a moment.

Her puzzled look made him continue. "I was just remembering when you were so excited to see a motel room because you'd never been in one before."

She chuckled. "Yes, I was very green back then. I've done a fair amount of traveling since then. You must have found me very boring."

"I found you adorable." His quiet statement caused a warm color to flow over her cheeks, which amused him.

"Hardly that, I'm sure. Looking back, I can better appreciate the patience you had in dealing with me. I was pretty headstrong."

"Was?" he repeated.

She grinned. He seemed to be coming out of his mood, if the teasing light in his eyes was any indication.

"I know I used to give you a bad time, Dane, but I didn't know how else to handle how I felt about you."

His eyes narrowed slightly, but he didn't say anything.

"I had such a crush on you, and was so afraid that you would find out. I suppose if I'd had a mother to talk to, or a sister, I would have been better able to handle my feelings for you. As it was, the only way I could find to cover it was with hostility and belligerence."

He sat back in his chair slightly and studied her. "Was that what all of your rebellion was about?"

She smiled. "Most of it. Part of it was growing pains, I'm sure."

"Well, the finished product was well worth it. You've turned into a pretty special person."

"Thank you, kind sir."

"I missed you," he said huskily. The tone of his voice and words tugged at her heartstrings.

"Is that why you called and wrote so much while I was gone?"

"You know me better than that. I doubt that I ever wrote a letter in my life."

"You could have called."

"And said...what? I miss you, please come home?"

Taking her courage in both hands, Felicia said softly, "If you had, Dane, I would have been home on the next flight."

Dane felt as though a sledgehammer had just hit him, knocking him senseless. He had known Felicia a long time and he had never seen her so serious, or so sincere. What she was telling him wiped out every thought in his brain. He could only sit there and stare at her in silence.

She took a sip of her wine, watching him. Dane looked stunned. Felicia felt a certain amount of satisfaction at having caught him so unaware. Deciding to follow up on her advantage, she suddenly asked him something she'd wanted to know for years.

"Why have you stayed single all these years?" Would he answer her, or would he tell her it was none of her business? And would he give her the answer she hoped to hear?

"I think you know," he said after a moment. "You have kept me single."

She tried to think of something light to say. "Are you saying I somehow managed to cramp your style during all this time? I've been gone for five years. You've had plenty of time to make up for what you might have lost because of me."

Dane shook his head, finished his drink and signaled the waiter to bring him another one. "You've never had a clue about how I felt about you, have you?"

"I thought I did, when you refused to make love to me that night. After what you said in the car earlier today, I now realize you have some very strong protective instincts where I'm concerned."

"That's true. I loved you too much to take advantage of the situation. I loved you too much to allow you to walk out of my life once I'd made love to you." He sat back and allowed the waiter to set his drink in front of him, pour Felicia more wine and walk away.

"And how do you feel about me now, Dane?" she asked, trying to hide the trembling that had begun deep inside her with his words.

"My feelings have never changed."

So now she knew, Felicia thought in wonder. Now she knew. And here they were, once again in a motel together, both consenting adults, and what were they going to do about it?

Probably nothing, thanks to Dane's code of honor. But was she ready for anything more? Loving Dane Rineholt had become such a habit to her that she hadn't considered what it would mean to have her love returned.

A light seemed to come on within her at the thought. To have Dane love her in return was a pleasure she needed to grow accustomed to. Knowing he loved her changed her perception of many things.

Dane nodded toward the dance floor, where several people were dancing to the music provided by a small band. "Would you care to dance?"

Silently she nodded and rose, and they walked out on the dance floor without speaking. Felicia turned and placed both her hands around his neck, so that he had no choice but to wrap his arms around her. The music was slow, the lights were low and Felicia knew that something important had shifted in her life during the past few moments. Not only had she been freed from the burdens of her past, but she had a glimpse into her future, a future that might be shared with Dane.

She rested her head on his shoulder and relaxed against him, letting her body flow into his, acknowledging to them both how well they fit together in so many ways.

Dane wondered if he enjoyed inflicting pain on himself. Holding Felicia in his arms was an exquisite form of torture. She no longer resisted him, as though his confession about his feelings had made a difference to her.

Until tonight he had always thought the attraction between them was one-sided. With Felicia's explanation, he realized that she had recognized her own feelings many years before.

Not that their feelings changed anything between them. She still had a career in California. His home would always be in Texas. But for a while, anyway, they could enjoy each other, enjoy being together.

By the time they returned to the table, they had communicated, nonverbally, how very much they wanted each other. Without a word Dane picked up the check, placed money with it and walked out of the restaurant with Felicia.

They walked up the wide stairway to the second floor, then down the hall to Felicia's room. Dane opened the door, but when Felicia went inside, he didn't follow.

"Would you like to come in?"

His lopsided smile almost made her melt. "Very much. But I'm not going to."

"Turning me down again, huh?" she said in a light tone.

"You should know better than that. Don't pretend you weren't aware out on that dance floor how very much I want you."

"But?"

"Nothing's changed, really. We need to keep our heads clear and not complicate matters. We've got to find Adam."

"Yes."

"So I'll meet you in the coffee shop tomorrow morning, eight o'clock, okay?"

She smiled. "Whatever you say."

"Don't look at me like that."

"Like what?"

"Like I'm a fool for not staying with you."

"You must be imagining that look, Dane. I wasn't thinking that at all." She chuckled. "I'm just continually amazed at your willpower."

"Now you're making fun of me."

"Dane?"

"What?"

She leaned up and kissed him softly on the mouth, her lips lingering slightly. Then she stepped back. "I love you," she said quietly, then closed the door.

Felicia turned away from the door, amazed at how tranquil she felt, considering all that had happened. Seeing Dane again after all these years had sharply brought into focus who he was and what he was. Would she love him as much if he didn't have such an iron self-control?

Well, maybe where I'm concerned, she admitted to herself with a grin. She had learned so much today—about him, about herself and about the possibility of their having a future together.

But first they had to find Adam.

Thinking of Adam reminded her of one of their last conversations before she moved. She could better understand now what Adam had been saying. But at the time she was too hurt and confused to grasp the message.

She had been home a week and she had made it clear she wanted nothing to do with Dane. Whenever he would walk into the room, she would suddenly remember business she had elsewhere. On this particular night, Dane had left right after supper, and she and Adam were in the living room. She'd been reading a magazine and he had been thumbing through a ranching journal.

"What are you going to do now that you've graduated, Sis?" Adam asked, looking up from his reading.

"Afraid I'm going to be a burden to you for the rest of your life?" she teased.

"Of course not! I wasn't sure if you intended to stay here and work at the paper again this summer, or whether you had some job interviews set up."

"I'm seriously considering a job offer I received, but I wanted to take the time to really think it through."

"Where is it?"

"Los Angeles."

"California?"

"Unless they've moved it. Why are you sounding so shocked?"

"I thought you'd want to work somewhere nearby."

"That thought had crossed my mind, but so far, no one is beating a path to my door, begging me to write for them."

"And if they did?"

"I'm not sure. Although I would consider it."

"What about Dane?"

Felicia felt herself stiffen at the name and she tried to look as casual as possible when she asked. "What about him?"

"I thought you and Dane would have come to some sort of an agreement by now."

"The only agreement we've ever reached is that we'll never agree about anything."

"But you're both in love with each other," he said in a quiet voice.

Oh, no. Had she been that obvious that even Adam had seen her feelings? She couldn't bear it if she had. Not after the way Dane had rejected her. "I can't imagine how you ever got that idea."

"Me, either. Must be something about having lived in the same house with the two of you for the past seven years and watched the tension build."

"That wasn't love, believe me. More like hate."

"You don't hate Dane, Felicia."

"Not really. But he has no use for me. He's made that plain."

"That's why he canceled the plans he made here in order to take you to that party in Austin a couple of weeks ago, I suppose."

"What plans?"

"Some friends invited him to go with them out to West Texas. He backed out at the last minute after you called."

Dane hadn't acted as though he'd had anything else to do when she had called. Funny that he hadn't told her.

"He was just being polite by agreeing to take me."

"Of course he was. Dane is so damned polite to people it's hard to believe."

They looked at each other for a moment, then burst out laughing. Anyone who knew Dane at all knew he didn't do anything he didn't want to do.

"Okay, so he put himself out to take me. That certainly doesn't mean he loves me."

"You think he doesn't?"

She remembered her humiliation in the motel. "I know very well he doesn't. He's made that quite clear."

"I see. Have you been holding out on me, little sister?"

She couldn't control the blush that seemed to overtake her. "Don't be ridiculous. Dane is ten years older than I am. He considers me much too young for him."

"Or maybe he thinks you feel he's too old for you."

"He knows better," she muttered.

"So you *are* in love with him, aren't you?"

She spun away from him and stomped over to the window. "What difference does it make? You and Dane are both confirmed bachelors." She looked over her shoulder. "Besides, it's not every woman's ambition to get married and raise a family."

"That's true. As I recall, you are determined to become a rich and famous writer."

"Maybe I will someday. You never can tell."

Adam walked over and put his arms around her. "I just want you to be happy, honey. No matter what you do or where you live. Be happy."

Felicia began to undress for bed, remembering that conversation and seeing how she had refused to hear what Adam was trying to tell her. Somehow he had known that Dane loved her, and was trying to help. "Be happy," he had said.

What was happiness? It wasn't something out there that a person could point to. It came from deep within, as a direct result of becoming comfortable with yourself.

It had taken Felicia several years to discover that truth. She had taken the job offer in Los Angeles. After two years she was offered a position on the staff of a brand-new women's magazine and she jumped at the opportunity.

She had tried to put Texas behind her, where it belonged, along with her adolescent yearnings for Dane. She had accomplished the goals she had set out to accomplish, but was she happy?

Remembering how she had felt in Dane's arms made her realize how empty her life had been, regardless of her professional success. She had proved something to herself by moving away and making it on her own. Perhaps that had been a necessary step in her growth. But she wanted more out of life. And Dane held the key to her future happiness, she felt certain.

As she slowly drifted off to sleep, Felicia drowsily acknowledged that Adam would be the first one to point out that he had known all along.

Five

Felicia woke up the next morning with a feeling of anticipation. She and Dane were going to Monterrey and they would find Adam, she was certain. They knew him better than anyone. If there was a clue to be found, between them they would find it.

By the time she reached the coffee shop, Felicia was bubbling with good feelings—until she saw Dane.

He sat in the far corner of the room, his back to the light, hunched over a cup of coffee. If he hadn't been wearing different clothes, she would have assumed he hadn't been to bed. He looked awful.

She slipped into the booth opposite him. "Good morning," she said quietly.

He flinched and raised his hand to his forehead. "Would you please speak a little softer?" he grumbled. He lifted his cup with a trembling hand.

"Are you okay?"

"I will be as soon as the aspirin I took takes effect."

She looked at him suspiciously. "If I didn't know better, I'd swear you have a hangover. But I don't see how two drinks could hit you like that."

He set his cup back down with care. "Simple. I had considerably more than two drinks. After I left you last night I went back to the bar."

"Oh."

"Is that all you can say? Oh?"

"What else do you want me to say?"

"You could point out what a stupid ass I am for drinking all night."

"Okay. Consider it said," she offered agreeably.

"Somehow that doesn't make the pain go away."

"I didn't think it would." Felicia was determined not to laugh. Never had she seen Dane look more vulnerable. His hair may have been combed earlier, but now it stood up in rumpled waves from his running his fingers through it. She had an almost uncontrollable urge to reach over and push it off his forehead. A hitherto unknown maternal instinct seemed to surge up inside her. "What were you celebrating last night?"

"Nothing. I thought I'd have a drink or two to help me sleep."

"And did they?"

"I can't remember."

She laughed and he winced. Quickly placing her hand over her mouth, she apologized. Hoping to tease him into a better frame of mind, she said, "What would Adam think of the example you're setting for his sister if he could see you now?"

Dane peered at her through slitted eyes. "I don't need to set any examples for you. You're a grown woman."

Her smile widened. "I'm glad you noticed. I thought you were still protecting me from myself last night."

"Hell, no. I was protecting me. There were no noble sentiments involved—purely self-preservation."

She knew it was unfair of her to take advantage of his feelings now that she knew how he felt about her. She wondered what, if anything, he intended to do about a future relationship.

"Have you ordered yet?" she asked, and watched as he turned even paler than before.

"No."

"Well, I'm going to have some breakfast. We have a long drive ahead of us." She gave her order to the waitress and hid her amusement as Dane ordered toast and more coffee. Served him right.

By nine o'clock they were across the border and headed south, with Dane grimly behind the wheel. Felicia had offered to drive, but he had waved her to the passenger side. She had decided not to argue, not with the mood he was in.

At least the weather had improved. Although cool, the day had turned out to be clear, and Felicia knew the sun would soon have the temperature climbing. Perhaps a warmer day might help to improve Dane's mood. She could only hope.

The drive to Monterrey along winding mountainous roads was tedious and tiring, even though the scenery was breathtaking. Felicia was grateful the rain had not followed them south. The roads would have been treacherous.

They stopped once to eat, then continued driving. The slight frown between Dane's brows disappeared as the day progressed, and Felicia hoped that was a sign he was feeling better.

She kept the conversation light, and when he didn't appear to want to talk she lapsed into silence.

When they arrived in Monterrey, Dane drove to the hotel where Adam had been staying at the time he'd disappeared. Dane explained to Felicia that he'd called from Laredo the night before and made reservations.

The hotel clerk was quite pleasant when they checked in, greeting Dane by name. Dane introduced her as Adam's sister.

"Ah, yes, Señorita St. Clair. We were so sorry to hear about your brother's disappearance. Have you heard anything about him?"

"No, not yet. We hoped that by coming down here, we might have a better chance of hearing something."

"Yes, it is hard to wait for word, I'm sure." He handed their keys to a young man hovering nearby. "Take their luggage on up, Jaime."

Catching the keys, the young man nodded, grabbed their bags, then headed toward the stairs. Dane and Felicia followed.

Jaime paused before two doors side by side. He opened each of them with a flourish and motioned them into the rooms. Felicia saw the connecting door, invitingly opened, into Dane's room as she walked into her own.

She watched while Dane tipped the bellman, then he disappeared from view. Walking over to the connecting door, she saw him standing in front of the windows.

"We shouldn't be disturbed by any street noises here," he said, looking out at a patio that resembled a fairyland of tropical flowers and greenery.

"No."

He glanced around. "I don't know about you, but I'm ready to get some sleep." He sounded almost defiant and she hid her smile of sympathy, knowing it wouldn't be appreciated.

She nodded. "That's a good idea for both of us, I think. Tomorrow is soon enough to make the rounds."

He looked so tired, and she loved him so much. She walked over to him and slid her arms around his waist. She just stood there, holding him for a moment, needing to feel his warmth.

Slowly he placed his hands on her back, as though his reluctance were being overcome by a compulsive need to touch her. They stood there in silence for several minutes, absorbing each other. Eventually Felicia leaned back so that she could see his face. He looked almost as though he were in pain—his eyes closed, his brows drawn into a frown.

She went up on tiptoes and kissed him softly. "Good night, Dane. I hope you sleep well." Slowly she pulled away from him. "I'll see you in the morning."

His arms tightened around her so that she couldn't move. "Don't go." His voice sounded harsh.

She knew what he was feeling because she felt it, too. How could she walk away from what they shared? All the years they had known each other had led to this moment. If she walked away he might never be in such a vulnerable mood again.

Somehow she had to let him know that he was more important to her than anything else. She loved him. She was more than willing to show him that love in its most physical form.

With an almost soundless sigh, Felicia put her arms around his neck and kissed him. Dane needed no more encouragement than that.

He picked her up in his arms and strode toward the bed. He needed her and he loved her. Forgotten were all his noble feelings of leaving her alone and letting her go. She was with him now and that was all that was important.

Their urgency swept them onto the bed. Dane couldn't get enough of the taste of her, giving her long, mind-drugging kisses that reached somewhere deep inside of her, curling her toes.

His iron self-control had deserted him, and as he tugged her clothes away from her, his mouth found new places to kiss, to touch, to taste.

Felicia felt as though she'd been caught up in a whirlwind of sensation. Everywhere he touched set off electrical charges that set her to quivering. But, then, so was he.

He paused, his hand brushing against her cheek. "Oh, Felicia. I never meant it to be this way." His ragged breathing stirred her as much as his trembling touch.

"It's okay, Dane. It's okay."

His mouth found hers once again, cutting off her words, and his hands began to memorize her body with quick strokes and lightning touches.

She felt his weight on her, pressing her into the bed, and she opened herself to him, holding him close as he made his entry.

A sharp pain shot through her, then was gone, to be replaced with a wonderful sense of completion, of wholeness, as though only now could she know what it had been she had yearned for all these years—to be possessed by Dane Rineholt.

She brought her thighs tightly around him, locking him into a fierce grasp that urged him to take her with him into the free-flowing world of sensual satisfaction.

His uncontrolled movement deep within her sparked flames that soon became infernos and Felicia suddenly cried out with the sudden riches unfolding before her. She felt as though sudden showers of color rained down around them, lighting the room with their brilliance.

And when Dane's arms tightened convulsively around her, a sudden spasm of deep contractions shook them both until they were limp.

Dane rolled onto his side, pulling her with him so that she remained firmly clasped in his arms, their legs still intimately entwined.

"I'm so sorry, love," he whispered. "So sorry."

Felicia heard the words but couldn't make sense of them, but she was almost too relaxed to say anything. "For what?" she finally murmured.

"For finally going over the edge...losing control...attacking you."

Felicia was still trying to regain her breath and her chuckle was shaky. "You didn't attack me, Dane. We're here in your room, after all.''

"I didn't mean to lose control."

"I'm glad you did." She reached up and smoothed the line between his brows. There was a sheen of perspiration on his face.

"But it was your first time."

"Yes."

"You should never have been rushed. I should have taken my time and—"

"It's okay, Dane. Really."

His eyes drooped close. "I haven't slept since you came back," he murmured. "I haven't been able to get you out of my mind since that night I almost made love to you. And, now..." His words faded away. He was asleep.

Felicia lay there, wrapped closely in his arms, and thought about what had just happened.

Dane had finally made love to her. And it had been even more wonderful than she had imagined. Perhaps there were other ways to go about lovemaking, but she could find no fault with the powerful way he had taken her across a new frontier.

Her eyes shifted shut and she, too, fell asleep.

* * *

When Dane woke up he was disoriented. There was no light in the room, but he knew he wasn't in his own bed. His arm felt strange, almost numb. When he tried to move it he discovered Felicia asleep by his side.

Memories flooded over him of what she was doing there and he had to bite off the curses that rose within him. He had finally lost his sanity, his control and his heart, not necessarily in that order.

Felicia moved closer and he realized why he'd awakened. The room's chill had finally gotten to them because they were on top of the covers. Like some madman he hadn't even taken time to pull the sheets and bedspread back before tossing her onto the bed and attacking her.

Carefully sliding his arm out from under her so that she wouldn't awaken, Dane got up and strode into the other room. Flipping on the light switch, he saw her suitcase at the end of her bed, waiting. He walked over and pulled back the covers, then went into the other room.

Lifting her gently, he carried Felicia into her room and placed her on the bed, then pulled the covers up around her. After carefully closing the door that separated their rooms, he went in and took a shower.

He had to decide what he was going to do now. He would be lying if he said he regretted what had happened, not when he'd wanted her for so many years. But not here. And not now, when both of their emotions were so torn because of Adam.

But he had to face facts. He'd made love to her and he'd made no effort to protect her against pregnancy. How irresponsible could a person be?

Dane stood under the shower and let the water beat down on him, almost as though he needed the punishment of the driving force against his body.

And now that he knew what making love to her was like how the hell was he going to manage to keep his hands off her? He felt as though a dam had burst inside him and all his overpowering emotions for Felicia had swamped him, until he was helpless before them.

He turned off the water, dried himself off and went back to bed, this time under the covers.

* * *

Bright sunlight beamed through the windows of the room and Felicia blinked against the glare when she first opened her eyes.

For a moment she didn't know where she was or why. Then she remembered the trip to Monterrey the day before. Only then did she remember what had happened once they'd gone to their rooms.

Glancing around, she realized she was in her bed, alone. The door that separated the rooms was closed. Shifting slightly, she became aware of her body and the fact that it was unclothed and slightly tender in various locations.

Dane must have brought her in here. She had no recollection of coming to bed. The last thing she remembered was that he had said *I'm sorry*.

She blinked away the sudden tears that came to her eyes. He had made gloriously passionate love to her—then apologized!

Felicia tried to swallow past the lump that formed in her throat. For whatever his reason, he was sorry. How could she deal with that?

Forcing herself up, she went in and showered, taking her time, trying to come to terms with the adjustments that would have to be made in their relationship.

After all, it wasn't the end of the world, was it? He might be sorry, but she wasn't. How could she be? She loved him. And he had said he loved her. So what was the problem?

Perhaps there wasn't one. Perhaps he had thought to save her some embarrassment by giving her some privacy this morning. She certainly hoped that was all it was. She would know soon enough.

Dressing carefully, Felicia made sure she looked her best before she went over and knocked on the connecting door. After a brief pause, she heard Dane's voice.

"It's open."

Not a particularly loverlike greeting.

Felicia opened the door and stepped into his room. He sat on the side of his rumpled bed, fully dressed, listening on the phone. He took one, all-encompassing glance at her and dropped his eyes to the pad and pencil in front of him.

"Okay, then give me what you have," he said into the phone.

Felicia watched as he took down whatever he was being told. Her eyes were drawn to the bed, where she had started out the evening. She could feel the warmth of her skin as she remembered how she had felt. Glancing at Dane, she noticed how his shirt stretched tautly across his back as he leaned forward, talking on the phone. She could almost feel the hard surface of his back rippling and flexing beneath her palms.

Jerking her gaze away, her eyes fell to where the material of his khaki pants tightened over his thigh and she could almost feel the sensation of his thigh between hers as it had been the night before.

Hurriedly looking away, she walked over to the window and stood staring at the profusion of greenery on the patio.

"All right. This will get us started," Dane said. "Felicia wants to put an ad in the paper, offering a reward for information." There was a pause, then he spoke again. "I know. I've thought of that. But we've got to do something to get some action. If this is all you've turned up in a week, we're in trouble."

She glanced over at the pad and noted a few lines of writing, but from where she stood couldn't decipher them.

"All right. But if you hear anything, call me at this number. Otherwise I'll get back with you tonight."

When he hung up he stood and looked at her with an intent gaze that gave her no clue as to his thoughts. "How are you feeling?"

She smiled. "I'm fine."

As though reluctant, he walked toward her, stopping in front of her. "You slept okay?" His husky voice always had such an effect on her.

She nodded, unable to say anything.

"We need to talk about last night, but not now. There's too much to do. But I do want you to know that you don't have to worry about anything. I'll take care of what needs to be done."

What was he talking about? What needed to be done? Before she could formulate a question, he asked, "Are you ready for breakfast?"

"Yes."

He motioned her to the door without a word.

They ordered breakfast, and while they waited, Dane pulled out the piece of paper he'd pulled off the pad and stuck in his pocket.

"I've been given the name of a man that may be of some help to us, but he might be hard to find."

"Who is he?"

"One of the best agents in the Mexican operations. Because he is who he is, he's next to impossible to trace, but if anyone can help us, Alvarez would be the man."

"So what do you suggest?"

He looked at her for several long moments without speaking. Then, as though making up his mind about something, he said, "Felicia, do you trust me?"

"Of course."

"Then will you accept my judgment when I tell you that the people I need to spend my time contacting will not meet me with you along? I need to go by myself. I would feel much better if you'd agree to stay here at the hotel and wait until I get back."

"How long do you think it will take?"

"I can't predict. Whether I have any luck or not, I'll try to get back here by midafternoon."

"Isn't there anything I can do during that time? I could at least go to the paper, talk to the police."

He thought about that for a moment, then nodded. "All right. See what you can find out. But be back here no later than noon, okay?"

"I'll do my best."

He sat there for a moment, studying her. With something like resignation he said, "I know you aren't going to like this, but I've spent a considerable amount of time thinking about it. Before you fly off the handle and tell me off, at least give the idea some thought."

"What idea?"

"I want us to get married as soon as I can make the arrangements down here."

Surely there were more romantic proposals made in this world? However, Felicia didn't care how it was worded when Dane Rineholt chose to discuss the subject.

Trying to sound as noncommittal as possible, she merely murmured, "Do you?"

He seemed to relax somewhat at her calm response. Taking her hand in his, he said, "It's the safest way I know to protect you at the moment, in many ways. You said you love me, and I believe that. You know how I feel about you. Under normal circumstances we wouldn't be in such a hurry, but I'm afraid that last night changes things. You weren't protected and I don't want to take a chance that you might be pregnant. If anything should happen to me, you'd have the protection of my name."

She studied him for a moment with a grave expression. "Are you afraid something is going to happen to you?"

"I'm certainly not counting on it. But we're into something dangerous now. I tried to explain that to you earlier and you said you were willing to face that danger."

"I am."

"Then allow me to do what I can."

"All right."

He seemed surprised to hear her easy acceptance. "This doesn't have to be permanent," he went on, effectively dashing the elation that seemed to be creeping over her.

"No?"

"Of course not. Once we find Adam and get out of here we can have the marriage annulled if you aren't pregnant. You'll be free to go back to L.A. and continue your life out there."

"And what will you do?"

"What I've been doing."

"Risking your life."

"That part doesn't matter. The main thing is, you'll be okay, no matter what happens."

Dane's intent gaze seemed to swallow and surround her. He had always protected her. Why was she surprised at his attitude now? But she didn't need his protection. She wanted his love. *He's giving you that, too, whether he acknowledged it or not,* she reminded herself.

"So what do we do now?" she asked.

He smiled for the first time since she'd walked into his room that morning. "Let's go find out how to get married."

Dane knew his way around the city. Within an hour he had found the necessary office to issue the necessary papers and they found a local official to officiate. Then he whisked her back to the hotel.

"Adam is certainly going to be surprised when he turns up," Felicia said as she got out of the car when they arrived back at the hotel.

Dane escorted her to their rooms without making a comment and left her at the door, saying, "I'll see you this afternoon."

The door closed behind him.

"Well. The new bride has been escorted to her suite and abandoned." She looked around the room and realized that they no longer needed two rooms. Calling down to the front desk, she told them she would not be using that room. Then she moved her things in with Dane, made sure the connecting door was locked on their side and headed out once again.

First, the newspaper office. Luckily she found someone to help her draw up a notice, but it took considerably longer than she had anticipated. Then she went to the police station.

After waiting almost half an hour, she was shown into the office of Lieutenant Delgado.

"How may I help you, Señora Rineholt?"

She loved the sound of that. In fact, it had given her a considerable amount of pleasure to announce her new name when she asked to speak to someone in charge.

"My brother, Adam St. Clair, was staying here in Monterrey last week and he is now missing."

"St. Clair. Yes, I believe I remember the name. Excuse me," he said, picking up the phone. He spoke into it in Spanish too rapid for her to begin to translate. When he hung up, he explained, "I've asked for the file."

She nodded.

"You have been here long?" he asked.

"No. My husband and I arrived last night."

"I see. This is too bad about your brother."

"Yes. Hopefully he's just been stranded somewhere out of reach of phones or something."

"Let us hope," Delgado replied. A young woman walked in, handed him a file, then left. He studied it for several moments in silence. When he looked up, his expression was grave. "Do you know why your brother was here in Mexico?"

"I was told he was here on business."

He glanced down. "Ah, yes. Business." He looked back at her, his black eyes very serious. "I'm afraid it's a very dangerous business your brother is doing here."

"Yes, I know."

"You know about it?"

"I only found out once he disappeared."

"There is another agency in our government that has taken over the investigation. They have agreed to keep us informed, but—" he shrugged "—who knows?" He closed the file. "I don't think I am going to be able to assist you, *señora.*"

Felicia stood up and held out her hand. "I appreciate your courtesy in seeing me, Lieutenant Delgado. If any news does turn up, I hope you will contact us at our hotel.''

"Certainly." His voice was grave and she shivered. He didn't expect to have any news. At least, not any good news.

Oh, dear God. His attitude forcibly confirmed Dane's concerns.

Felicia hurried back to the hotel. No doubt Dane had returned by now and would not be happy that she had taken so long. Her mind worried over the existing facts and what she and Dane could do now that they were in Monterrey. She was so caught up in her thoughts that she didn't see the man until he stepped up beside her.

"Señorita St. Clair?"

Startled, she glanced up. "Yes?" She stared into the dark eyes of a man not much taller than she was. Without another word he grasped her arm and shoved her into the backseat of a car parked alongside the curb.

Six

The wide seat of the limousine easily held its three passengers. With as much dignity as possible, Felicia managed to seat herself, finding a place between the other two occupants.

She could not remember ever having been so frightened. Her discussion with the police hadn't helped calm her imagination, either. Were these people somehow connected to Adam and his disappearance?

"Who are you?" she asked, wishing her voice didn't sound quite so shaky.

"No es importante," was the answer.

It might not be important to you, she thought, hoping they couldn't see how frightened she was, *but I'd like to know what's going on.*

"Where are you taking me?"

Her question was greeted with silence.

She had to remind herself that the laws, rules and regulations of the United States did not apply at the moment. How could she explain to them that they couldn't just drag someone off the street and take her somewhere, when they had just done it?

She looked out the window, trying to get her bearings. Nothing looked familiar. The car was moving away from the central part of the city out into the residential area. She wondered if she'd have to find her way back. Glancing at her captors without trying to call attention to the fact, she noted that they were of obvious Mexican heritage, small and dark, and that they looked no different than most of the people she'd seen since they arrived.

So much for trying to give a description.

She thought of Dane and wondered what he would do when he returned to the hotel and found her gone. He would not be pleased, that was clear. Certainly he would realize that she'd be there if she could, but that wouldn't be of much consolation to him. As far as he knew, she had mysteriously disappeared.

Just like Adam.

Was it possible she was going to be taken to Adam? At least she would know he was all right.

The limousine turned into a driveway and waited while a wrought-iron gate opened slowly. Then it drove through and followed a winding driveway through trees and around hills until it came to a stop before a house that was so large it looked as though it sprawled over several acres.

With a courtesy that had been lacking up until now, the men stepped out of the car and assisted her out. They nodded toward the front entrance for her to precede them, then flanked her as she walked up the steps.

When the door swung open at her approach she almost giggled, and realized the strain was getting to her. Hadn't she seen a scene similar to this on some television adventure series?

Her escorts ushered her into a room that was large enough for a football scrimmage, nodded and left, closing the double doors behind them.

It was only when she took a few more steps into the room and looked around that she discovered she was not alone.

"Come in, Señorita St. Clair."

A slight, elderly man rose from a chair behind a majestic desk and strode across the Persian rug to where she stood. She could only stare mutely at him. Whatever was going on, someone forgot to explain her part in it.

"Please, won't you sit down?" He motioned to a comfortable chair. "Would you like some coffee, perhaps, or tea?" His face was a deep teak color; his hair, an iron gray, was brushed back from his face. He looked very distinguished.

"Who are you?" she finally managed to say.

He smiled, motioning her to a chair. She forced herself to walk the few steps and sit down, poised on the edge of the chair.

"Allow me to introduce myself. I am Felipe Santiago. I thought, of course, that you would know that, or you would never have accepted my invitation to visit."

"I didn't receive an invitation, Mr. Santiago. Your men forced me into a car and brought me here."

He frowned slightly. "There must be some mistake."

"I would agree to that," she said wryly.

"Please forgive me. I had no idea. I asked them to deliver a message to your hotel that if it was convenient, I would like to speak with you regarding your brother."

Forgotten was the manner in which she had arrived. His words had wiped the previous half hour from her mind. "Do you know where Adam is?" she asked eagerly.

"Unfortunately I do not. However, I do know your brother quite well, and I was most concerned to learn that his whereabouts are not known at the moment."

"Do you know what he was doing down here?"

"I believe Adam had several business interests in the area. We generally have dinner together whenever he comes to Mexico."

"Did you see him on this trip?"

"Yes, as a matter of fact we had dinner the first evening he was here."

"Did he tell you where he was going?"

"Not really, no."

She sat back, disheartened. For a little while she had thought she might have found a lead.

"I would not worry about your brother if I were you, Señorita St. Clair. I believe he can take care of himself."

"I know. But I've been so worried."

"That is understandable." He glanced around when the door opened and a young man in a white coat and black trousers walked in, carrying a tray with a large silver service on it. "Some coffee, perhaps?"

She nodded.

Felipe motioned for the tray to be placed on the table in front of her. She picked up the heavy silver pot and poured coffee into a beautifully made china cup. When she offered it to the man seated across from her, he shook his head.

"How long do you intend to stay here in Monterrey, Señorita St. Clair?"

"Actually, my name is Rineholt, Mr. Santiago. My husband and I aren't sure how long we'll stay. Hopefully until we can find Adam."

Felipe sat very still and stared at her. "Dane Rineholt is your husband?" he asked in a neutral tone.

She smiled. "Yes. Do you know Dane?"

"No. However, Adam often speaks of him. They are partners, I believe."

"Yes."

"He has never mentioned that the two of you are married."

"There was no reason for him to mention it, I'm sure."

"No," Felipe agreed thoughtfully, "I don't suppose there was." He was silent for several minutes while she politely sipped on her coffee and wondered how she was going to get away. Dane was probably frantic by now.

Felipe tugged at his bottom lip for a moment, then, as though coming to a decision, he stood. "Well, I could not have Adam's sister and partner remaining at a hotel when they could be here with me. Both of you must accept my hospitality and stay here while you are in Monterrey."

Felicia also stood. "Oh, no. We can't do that. As a matter of fact, I'm sure Dane is quite worried by now. I was supposed to have met him back at the hotel several hours ago. I really need to—"

"Nonsense. I insist on your staying here. I will call your husband and have him meet us here for dinner."

"But—"

"Please do not feel you are imposing. I have more than enough room." Felipe started toward the door, then paused. "Come. I will show you."

Felicia slowly followed him out of the room, to find him waiting by the ornate stairway that curved to the second floor. Lightly grasping her elbow, he escorted her up the stairs.

She couldn't decide what to do. He was being polite, but she couldn't get rid of the feeling that he was no friend of Adam's, no matter what he had to say.

They passed along a hallway with several closed doors. At the end of the hall, Felipe opened the door and motioned for her to step inside.

The room was enormous, with windows on two sides. An oversize bed occupied only a small portion of the interior, and part of the room was utilized as a sitting room. "It's beautiful," she said truthfully.

Felipe nodded graciously. "Thank you. I believe you will be most comfortable here, Señora. I'm sure you must be tired. If you would like to rest, feel free.''

Did she have a choice? He had been quite arbitrary in everything he had said and done. She walked a few steps more into the room and heard the door close behind her. Whirling around, she heard the distinct click of the lock.

Her kind host had just locked her inside the room.

Dane had not made the connections as quickly as he'd hoped, but he had gotten a great deal of information in a few hours. There was no doubt that Adam had been involved in a big drug buy. Playing himself, Adam had convinced the necessary parties that his position as a rancher was a perfect cover for dealing in large quantities of drugs.

With his legitimate business interests south of the border, Adam had a perfectly good reason for traveling between the two countries.

Someone had bought the story.

None of the people in Monterrey who knew Dane knew his connection with Adam. Dane had been around for years and his drug contacts felt safe with him. So they were complaining about the new man coming down and muscling in on the business.

Adam's disappearance could have been caused by several different factions.

Dane would need to follow up some of the leads before he was sure the group he was currently working with hadn't been the ones responsible.

Dane didn't know what he was going to tell Felicia. The news was not good. Since no one had seen or heard from Adam since the day he'd disappeared, chances were good that he had been killed the same day.

Otherwise there would be some hint of his whereabouts.

No one seemed to know anything.

Dane strode down the hall to his room—correction, their room. Knowing Felicia's temper, she was probably mad as hell that he had been gone so long. He grinned. The situation had changed considerably from the years when he'd had to be an adult to her child. She was definitely an adult now. And his wife.

He opened the door to his room, not too surprised to find it empty. He tried the connecting door and discovered it had been locked. Unlocking it, he threw open the door and walked into the other room. The bed was made up and the room empty. None of her things were there.

What the hell?

He spun around and went back into his room and slammed the door. Going over to the phone, he called the front desk.

"This is Dane Rineholt."

"Yes, *señor*?"

"Where is Miss St. Clair?"

"I do not know, sir."

"None of her things are in her room."

"No, sir. She said she would no longer need the room."

"I see," he said, and hung up the phone slowly.

He should have known. She had been entirely too docile this morning, agreeing to the marriage without an argument, agreeing that he should check on his leads alone.

But where could she be? He got up and went into the bathroom for a drink. Reaching for a glass, he froze. Her toiletries were neatly set out next to his razor, brush and comb.

He walked back into the bedroom. Her suitcase was next to his. Dane took a deep breath and relaxed. Of course. There was no reason to keep two rooms. She had moved into his. He realized that his heart was racing. He'd been scared she had left him.

He laughed, the sound loud in the quiet of the room. They'd only been married a few hours and he already expected problems.

But where the hell was she?

He paced the floor, wondering whether to go look for her or stay at the hotel in case she came back shortly. Perhaps she'd run out to buy something. Or maybe she'd gone downstairs to eat. She could be anywhere.

Making a sudden decision, he walked over and called the desk, asked for the number of the police station, then phoned there. After explaining three different times that he was looking for Felicia St. Clair, he was finally connected to Lieutenant Delgado.

"Yes, Señor Rineholt?"

"I'm looking for my wife," Dane stated baldly.

"I see. And you do not know where she is?"

"Not at the moment, no. She had planned to go to the police and I wondered—"

"Señora Rineholt was here earlier in the day, but that was several hours ago."

"I see."

"Your wife is a very courageous woman, *señor*."

"I know."

"She may have need of that courage."

"You don't think Adam's alive, do you?"

"No, *señor*. And neither does anyone else who's working on the case."

Dane rested his head against his hand. "I know." Defeat was noticeable in his voice.

"Have you prepared Señora Rineholt for that possible outcome?"

"I haven't dwelled on it, no. I don't want to destroy her hope unnecessarily. And there's always that chance—"

"*Señor*, you and I can be honest with each other. Señor St. Clair has chosen a very dangerous occupation. He knew at the time that there was very little anyone could do to help him if he got into trouble."

"Did you know Adam?"

"No, but he worked very closely with a man whom I've known for years. He said Adam was one of the best. He knew the risks, and he was willing to take them."

"I know."

"His sister must be made to understand. We all do what we can. The rest is left up to God."

"Look, I'd better get off the phone. Felicia may be trying to reach me. I'll keep in touch. If you hear anything, let me know."

"Of course. Oh, and Señor Rineholt?"

"Yes?"

"You have a very lovely wife. Take care of her."

"That's what I'm trying to do, but so far I haven't been very successful."

"Don't worry. I'm sure she'll be there soon."

Dane hung up the phone and stretched out on the bed. Delgado was right. He needed to prepare Felicia for the probable outcome of their search. There was a very good chance that no word would ever be heard of Adam again. A body could be easily hidden in the surrounding mountains and never discovered.

Dane hadn't realized how much he had come to accept the fact that Adam was gone. The longer the time went by with no word, the more certain he had become.

Adam was well trained. If there had been any way for him to get a message to Dane, he would have. The silence was ominous.

The sudden ringing of the phone caused Dane to start. He grabbed it before it could ring again.

"Rineholt."

"Are you interested in seeing your pretty wife again, *señor*?" a voice said softly.

Dane's worst fears had just been put into words. He felt as though a giant hand had squeezed his heart. "Yes," he said, trying not to show any emotion.

"Then you will follow my instructions."

"Yes," he repeated.

The voice began to tell Dane where to go, following a series of back streets with many twists and turns. And he was advised not to notify the police.

But the police already know I'm looking for her, he thought.

"When you reach that location, stay in your car. You will be met."

"Will Felicia be there?" he asked.

"Come alone," was his only answer before the other man hung up.

First Adam, now Felicia. Why had he allowed her to talk him into bringing her to Mexico? He should have insisted she stay at the ranch. He should have— He should— Dane jumped up and, grabbing his coat, headed for the door.

He had to face reality, whether he liked it or not.

The directions were detailed and obviously set up to be sure that he was not being followed. Dane had a strong hunch that someone was watching him from the time he left the hotel. It didn't matter. Nothing mattered but finding Felicia. The city lights did not extend out as far as he was directed to go and dark shadows decorated the tree-lined streets with scallops and ribbons of black. When he got to the designated area, he discovered a little park that would, no doubt, be beautiful in daylight.

He pulled up and parked, then switched off his headlights. Checking the time, he realized he was early. Did they intend to bring her to him? Was she out there in the park somewhere alone? Hurt? Dane tried not to guess what could be happening to her.

A car turned onto the street ahead of him and slowly approached. When it was even with his car, it stopped and the window was rolled down.

"Dane Rineholt?"

"Yes."

The back door opened. "Get in."

He didn't need a second invitation. Dane got out of the car and crawled into the other one. The backseat was empty.

Two men sat in front. As soon as the door closed behind him, the car sped away.

"Where's Felicia?"

The man who had spoken to him glanced around. "You'll know soon enough."

The car seemed to get lost in a maze of streets, coming out eventually into a well-kept neighborhood with high walls and curving driveways. They turned into one of the drives. He noted that wrought-iron gates closed behind them as soon as they passed.

When they pulled up in front of the house, Dane looked at it in surprise. The home, with its white adobe walls and red tile roof, could have been a villa on the Mediterranean.

He was escorted inside and left in a wide hallway with a curving staircase that disappeared upstairs. Was Felicia here?

A young man in dark pants and a white coat appeared, carrying a large tray covered with food.

"Señor Rineholt?"

"Yes."

"Follow me, please."

Dane followed him up the staircase, wondering whose home they were in. "Whose home is this?"

"Señor Santiago's, *señor*."

Dane had never heard the name. He had a feeling it was going to be very important to him.

"Where are you taking me?"

The man paused in front of a door at the end of the hallway, shifted the tray to his shoulder and unlocked the door. "Your room, *señor*," he said, opening the door and walking inside with the tray.

Dane followed him inside.

Felicia stood by a far window, looking out.

"Felicia!"

She had turned when the door opened, but when she saw the waiter she had returned her gaze to the window, wondering where she was and if she would ever be able to see Dane or Adam again.

When she heard Dane's voice she thought she was dreaming. Spinning around, she saw him stride across the room toward her.

"Oh, Dane!" She threw herself into his arms, and he held her as though he never intended to let her go. Neither one of them heard the door close behind the young man who had brought in the tray.

Cupping her face in his hands, Dane let his eyes wander over her face, as though memorizing every feature. Then his mouth found hers in a searing kiss that left them both shaken.

"Dear God!" Dane managed to mutter in a husky voice. "I've never been so scared in my life." His hands roamed over her back and shoulders, as though he were reassuring himself that she was all right.

From the safety of Dane's arms, Felicia could now admit to herself how frightened she had been. She could feel her legs shaking, and tightened the grip she had around his waist.

He picked her up and carried her to the bed, gently placing her in the center and sinking down beside her, still holding her closely in his arms.

"Are you all right?" he asked with concern, brushing a wisp of hair off her forehead.

She nodded. "Now that you're here."

The expression in her eyes caused a trembling deep inside him. He fought to control the strong surge of passion that swept over him, but when Felicia gently tugged on his neck, bringing his mouth down to hers, he knew he was lost.

Dane never remembered later how they managed to dispose of their unwanted clothing. All he knew was the feel of her silky skin against him. His earlier tortured thoughts gave him cause to celebrate their closeness. He had feared that he might never see her again, feel the warmth of her body pressed against him, taste the sweetness of her mouth, touch the fullness of her breast that now filled his hand.

He loved her and he'd almost lost her. Dane never wanted to go through such agony again.

Felicia responded to his fierce lovemaking with equal fervor, her hands delicately stroking across his wide, muscular back, while his tongue gently caressed the pink tip of her breast.

Even that particular intimacy wasn't close enough to suit Dane and he shifted so that he was moving over her, nudging her legs apart. His mouth claimed hers once again, his tongue surging between her lips as he possessed her body. Felicia tightened her hold on him, clamping her thighs tightly and wrapping her arms around his shoulders.

Dane couldn't seem to get enough of the feel of her, the taste of her, the evocative scent that was so individually hers, and he clung to her with quiet intensity.

Felicia quickly recognized the sensations that began to wash over her in ever increasing waves as those feelings that Dane's lovemaking had introduced to her the night before. She'd had no idea her body could respond to another person that way. Perhaps she felt this way because she was with Dane. All she knew was she had been transformed into a creature of emotion and sensation, her body responding to him without thought or conscious direction.

The steady rhythm Dane set soon had them gasping, but he wouldn't pause. He had a driving need to claim her as his, to celebrate life and to overcome any possible fears of separation.

Felicia's eyes flew open, shocked at the intensity of the convulsive moves her body made as Dane's relentless strokes drove her first to the brink, then far over the edge of pleasure and satisfaction.

Her reaction caught Dane off guard, and his body reacted to hers by imitating its release. He groaned with the force of his final lunge, collapsing beside her, his chest heaving in his efforts to get air to his lungs.

Felicia smiled to herself as she gazed at him. His eyes were closed and she wondered if he had fallen asleep. A slight film of perspiration covered his brow and she reached up and pushed back the hair that fell across his forehead.

His eyes flickered open and he stared at her for a moment in silence. He traced her cheekbone with his forefinger, then whispered, "Are you okay?"

She smiled. "I'm fine."

He closed his eyes for a moment, then opened them again. "I don't think I'm ever going to let you out of my sight again."

"At this point, I'm not ready to argue with that."

He glanced around the bed ruefully. "I did it again."

"Did what?"

"Threw you on the bed without even bothering with the covers." He shook his head. "I seem to lose all control when I'm around you." He glanced around the room, then back at her. "How did you get here, anyway?"

"I was on my way back to the hotel from the police station, when a man called me by name, grabbed my arm and pushed me into a car. When I arrived, Felipe Santiago introduced himself and said he was a friend of Adam's. Then he started asking me about Adam and his disappearance."

"Did he say why he kept you here?"

"No. He just insisted that we stay here with him."

"How did he know we were married?"

"I told him. He seemed surprised."

Dane shifted slightly, but not enough to dislodge their legs from their entwined position. "No wonder. Did you tell him how long we'd been married?"

"I didn't think that was anyone's business. I'm not sure what it was, but something gave me the feeling that our being married didn't fit in with his plans." Felicia rubbed her hand lightly across his chest.

"I hope that works in our favor," he said, grabbing her fingers and bringing them to his lips, where he slowly kissed the tip of each one. "So far the marriage hasn't proven to be much of a protection for you."

"It has if that's the reason you're here," she responded. "How did you know where to find me?"

"I didn't. I got a phone call to meet someone and they brought me here."

Felicia was quiet for a few moments. "Did you find out anything about Adam?" she finally asked.

"Nothing encouraging, I'm afraid."

"What do you mean?"

"I mean that as soon as we can get away from here, we need to get back across the border as fast as we can."

"Dane! Does that mean..." She didn't seem to be able to finish her question.

"There's no way to know, Felicia. But our being in Mexico isn't helping anything. We've stumbled into a real mess. I should have known better than to bring you down here in the first place."

She met his steady gaze with her own. "You had no choice."

"I know. You are one of the most stubborn women I know," he said with a slight smile.

Her chin lifted slightly. "In a man, the trait would be called 'determined.'"

He sighed, rolling away from her and sitting up on the side of the bed. "Either way it's dangerous and I want to get you out of here."

He got up from the bed and walked over to the window. Hidden lights lit up the lawn. He stood there for a moment, ignoring his lack of clothing as he gazed out the window. "What were you watching out here earlier?"

Felicia leaned up on one elbow. "The dogs. I saw three of them."

Without looking around, he muttered, "I suppose it's too much to hope that they're someone's pets."

"They were Dobermans."

"I had a hunch they wouldn't be Chihuahuas. So if we manage to get out of this room, we still have to get off the property in one piece."

Wrapping the spread around her, Felicia joined him at the window. "I don't think Santiago intends to hurt us, Dane. I got the impression that he's trying to find out how much we know about Adam and why he was down here."

"And from all indications, he's not going to give us a chance to find out, either," Dane added, pulling her next to him.

She rested against his long length. "Other than the locked door, he's treated me with courtesy. He invited me downstairs for dinner, but I told him I wasn't feeling well, so he had dinner sent up."

"Are you feeling all right now?"

"Yes. It's amazing how quickly my health improved when you walked through the door."

Dane glanced over at the table. "Do you suppose we should eat?"

Felicia's gaze followed his. "It's probably cold by now, but it doesn't matter. I'm not all that hungry, are you?"

He shook his head. "But I could use a shower. Is there one available?"

Felicia stepped back with a smile. "Oh, yes. We have all the conveniences of home." She walked over to one of the doors and opened it, revealing a luxuriously appointed bathroom with a large shower stall as well as a tub.

Dane needed no more encouragement. He disappeared into the other room and turned on the water.

Felicia walked over and looked at the tray of food. She nibbled on a piece of salad, then poured herself a cup of coffee. After a sip of the lukewarm liquid she made a face and set the cup back on the tray. She glanced over her shoulder toward the bathroom.

Succumbing to impulse, she dropped the spread she had wrapped around herself like a sarong and walked into the bathroom and opened the shower door.

Dane glanced around, startled, then grinned when she closed the door behind her and picked up the bar of soap.

"I got lonesome," she explained solemnly as she began to soap his back.

"I certainly can understand the feeling," Dane responded with a smile. He turned around and, taking the soap from her, began to lather her body lovingly, from neck to thighs, with a gentle touch that had her trembling in minutes.

The warm water falling over Dane and her smoothed the lather away, leaving them both glistening with moisture. Dane's gaze seemed to burn her skin wherever it touched. Without taking his eyes off her or saying a word, he reached over and turned off the water.

Opening the shower door, Dane stepped out, picked up a towel and began to dry her. She stood there before him, already aroused by his touch, and watched him as he dried himself. Then he picked her up and carried her into the other room.

When Dane reached the bed he stood her on her feet and smiled. "This time I intend to do this right." He reached past her and pulled the covers down to the foot of the bed.

Then he picked her up and placed her on the center of the bed.

"This is our wedding night, you know," Felicia murmured.

"I'm very much aware of that fact," he replied. He propped himself up on one elbow beside her, studying her expression, and she smiled—a slow, tantalizing smile that increased the beat of his already racing heart. Dane placed his hand on her cheek and stroked it lightly with his finger, then ran his hand down her body until it came to rest at the top of her thighs.

Her body seemed to be ultrasensitive since their earlier lovemaking and Felicia felt as though a singed path was imprinted on her, marking every place he touched her.

"Did I hurt you earlier?" he asked quietly.

"No," she whispered.

"I seem to lose all control when I'm with you. You're so warm and passionate, so responsive."

"Only with you. I never wanted anyone else. And when I believed that you didn't want me, I knew I'd never discover what lovemaking was like."

"Not want you!" His hand clenched over her abdomen, then let go, stroking the soft flesh he found there. "I've lost count of the sleepless nights I've spent wanting you."

"Isn't this better than spending the evening drinking?"

"You'd better believe it. I know better than to try to forget with that method again. But I thought I was going to explode in Laredo. I had to do something, or I would have been beating on your door at three in the morning."

"I wouldn't have minded."

"Oh, you made that quite clear. I don't know why I felt I had to be so damned noble."

"For the same reason you married me . . . to protect me."

His hand began to trace a trail along her body, circling her breasts, then her navel, moving finally down to the short curls below her abdomen. Felicia had trouble concentrating on the conversation.

She reached out and caressed his chest, then slowly let her fingers slide down until they touched his aroused masculinity. Felicia heard him catch his breath and smiled.

"I married you because I love you," he said in an uneven voice.

"That's why I married you, too, you know." She leaned over and placed her mouth on his chest, kissing him lightly, touching her tongue to the nipple that was almost hidden in the tight curls surrounding it.

As though he could no longer tolerate what she was making him feel, he held her against him as he rolled over onto his back, so that her body blanketed him. "Oh, Felicia. I'll never get enough of you—your touch, your presence or your love in my life," he murmured, hungrily searching for her mouth.

Their slow, relaxed lovemaking escalated into a fiery need for both of them. Dane's hands wrapped around her waist in a firm grip and he lifted her slightly, fitting her to him, before surging upward, deep inside her.

Felicia almost cried out with the wonder of his aggressive possession. He felt so good to her, strong and hard, and she luxuriated in the feeling that they belonged together. They had waited so many years for this magic, but it had been worth the wait, the tears and the growing up.

She could hold her own with this man now. They were equals. At the moment she enjoyed the sense of being in control, even if for a few moments, as she set a pace for them in the ancient ritual of lovemaking.

Dane could take only so much before he pulled her down to his chest and hung on to her while he rolled over, placing her beneath him. She smiled up at him, noticing the tiny furrow between his brow, the slight dampness of his face, the look of concentration he wore that caused her to lose what little control she'd managed to salvage.

She clamped her thighs tighter around his hips, meeting each of his movements with one of her own, recognizing the sense of exultation that swept over her when she could tell he no longer maintained control over his reactions.

Then she was lost to everything but sensation. She felt as though she were in the midst of a celestial collision, with thousands of stars spinning out of control, sparkling the air all around them with myriad bits of color.

Dane's final lunge seemed to carry them away from earth's gravity, causing them to drift in that mindless space of utter contentment, causing them to fall into an exhausted sleep.

Yet during the night Dane reached for her again and again, to make sure she was there with him, to touch her hand and feel the reality of the ring on her finger, to stroke her breast, to kiss her slightly swollen lips and to ignite the flame within her once again.

When Dane woke up the next morning, he glanced around the large, airy room, trying to figure out where he was. Shifting his head slightly on the pillow, he saw Felicia sound asleep a few inches away. She looked very peaceful in her sleep, very much like the young girl he'd first met twelve years ago.

God, how he loved her! And he was going to do everything he could to protect her. Moving carefully so as not to wake her, he crawled out of bed and went into the bathroom. After a quick shower he put on the clothes he'd worn the day before, looked in the mirror and recognized that he needed to shave. There wasn't a hell of a lot he could do about that at the moment.

He decided to try the door, and discovered that it wasn't locked, so he went in search of his host. It took him several minutes to find his way to the dining room. Pausing in the open doorway, he watched as a gray-haired man stood up from behind the table and said, "Good morning, Señor Rineholt. I trust you slept well. Won't you join me for breakfast?"

Dane wondered if Alice had felt something similar after stepping through the looking glass. This affable man was the same one who had abducted Felicia and spirited him to his home?

Felipe poured another cup of coffee and set it at the place to his left at the long, ornate table. "Allow me to introduce myself. My name is Felipe Santiago. I happen to be an old friend of Adam St. Clair's."

"So Felicia said. He's never mentioned your name."

"Is that so? I'm surprised. He often speaks of you. He's quite fond of you, I think."

"We're very close."

"Of course. That is only natural, your being his partner as well as his brother-in-law."

"I suppose." Dane took a sip of the coffee, which was excellent. "Look, would you mind telling me what's going on?"

Felipe smiled. "I suppose you are a little confused, eh?"

"That's one way of putting it."

Felipe's face sobered. "Señor Rineholt. You and your wife have no business down here at the moment. In my own way I have tried to protect you. You are asking questions in places where the answers are fatal. Rather than try to reason with you, I chose to protect you in my own way, by bringing you here."

"Do you know where Adam is?"

"No. But I have reason to believe that he is dead."

Hearing the words spoken with such certainty was like a blow to Dane's solar plexus. "Did you kill him?" he managed to ask.

"Of course not. We were doing business together. Working with Adam, I stood to make a great deal of money. We both were. What I am afraid happened is that someone caught a scent of the money and insisted on getting in on it."

Dane realized that Santiago didn't know Adam was an agent, which meant that Santiago was one of the men trafficking in drugs. How ironic that they should get protection, of sorts, from someone who was probably one of the biggest dealers around, if his wealth was any indication.

"I appreciate what you're trying to do, but I don't really think it's necessary."

"Take my word for it, it's necessary. Your wife mentioned talking with the police yesterday. What did they tell her?"

"Nothing. They know nothing." He studied the man sitting there so relaxed. He looked like an average businessman with a receding hairline and a slight paunch. "What makes you believe Adam is dead?"

"Otherwise he would have contacted me. I feel certain that he was double-crossed by someone he trusted—someone, perhaps, we both trusted."

"Where does that leave you?"

"Without a means to sell what I am holding, but I have other avenues to pursue, as you well know."

"What do you mean?"

"I know who you are, Señor Rineholt. Your name keeps coming up whenever I am looking for another distribution source. You and Señor St. Clair are beginning to make a name for yourselves down here as free-spending Texans. I thought perhaps we could talk business while you are visiting with me."

"I wouldn't mind if my wife weren't here. She knows nothing about all this, and I want to keep her out of it."

"How do you propose to do that?"

"By taking her back home."

"I don't understand why you brought her in the first place."

"Because she wanted to find her brother."

"She won't find him."

"I believe that now. So I intend to take her back home."

"You're a very intelligent man, Señor Rineholt."

Dane held the other man's gaze. "If you'll help me get my car and return to the hotel, we'll be headed back to the border before noon."

Felipe nodded. "I believe that can be arranged. If you will give me your car keys, I will see that the car is delivered to the hotel. And my car will be available for you to leave at your convenience."

Dane stood up. "Thank you. I appreciate your concern for our safety. Other than scaring us out of our minds, we've had a very pleasant stay with you."

"I apologize for the manner in which I handled the matter, but it was the most expedient way, you understand."

"I understand." Dane left the dining room, determined to get Felicia and leave immediately.

When he opened the door to their bedroom he was relieved to find her dressed and seated at the table, sipping coffee. He leaned down and kissed her hard on the lips.

"Good morning. Are you ready to get out of here?" he asked.

Her eyes widened. "You mean he's going to let us leave?"

"Yes. Whenever we want."

Hastily setting the cup down, she stood. "Then let's go."

Dane pulled her into his arms and kissed her again. "We're going home today," he said, pulling away slightly.

"But what about Adam?"

"First things first. I'm going to get you out of this mess. Then I'll look for Adam."

He kept his arm around her shoulders and escorted her out of the room and down the stairs. When he opened the front door, a black limousine sat waiting at the bottom of the steps, with a chauffeur standing nearby.

"Shouldn't we say anything to Mr. Santiago?"

"Consider it said," Dane muttered. "Let's go."

They rode back to the hotel in silence. Felicia wished she knew what had caused the grim expression on Dane's face. He looked almost haggard. Of course, neither of them had gotten much sleep the night before.

She touched the ring that he had placed on her finger the day before and asked the ques-

RETURN TO YESTERDAY

tion that had popped into her head during her long, lonely wait.

"When did you find time to buy this ring, Dane?"

"I've had it in my wallet for some time."

"Was it an heirloom?"

"No. I bought it a couple of years ago."

"Oh." She probably didn't want to know the answer, but couldn't leave the subject alone. "Why?"

He'd been staring out the side window during most of their conversation, but he turned at her last question. With a wry smile he took her hand and rubbed the ring with his finger. "I had it in mind to fly out to L.A. and demand that you marry me and come back to Texas. I wanted the ring to show you I meant business."

"Then why didn't you?"

"Because after thinking it through, I knew I didn't want to force you into doing something you basically didn't want to do."

"As if you could," she scoffed lightly.

"That's what I did to you yesterday."

"Don't be silly. I married you because I wanted to marry you, and for no other reason."

"What about an annulment?"

"No way."

He began to smile. "You mean I'm stuck with you?"

"You got it, cowboy. That'll teach you, trying to wriggle out of a commitment."

"Not me, honey. I can think of nothing I like more than being married to you." He glanced out the window again. "I suppose I could divide my time between Texas and California. If you got used to city living, I'm sure I can, too."

"Do you mean that?"

He looked back at her. "Of course."

"I thought you expected me to give up my job."

"No. What I realized is that I wanted to be with you, no matter what. The ranch is important to me, but no more important than you are."

"And I've come to realize that my job is important, but no more important than you are."

He gripped her hand for a moment, then slowly relaxed his fingers, until they once again began to stroke hers. "We'll work it out someway."

She laid her head on his shoulder. "Adam's going to be so pleased," she said with a sigh.

Dane couldn't respond.

When they walked across the lobby the clerk motioned to them. Dane guided Felicia over to the desk.

"Your car keys were delivered a few moments ago, Señor Rineholt. Your car has been serviced for you."

"Thank you." He took the keys and dropped them into his pants pocket. Pulling the room key out of the same pocket, he continued down the hallway until reaching their room.

When he unlocked the door, he pushed it open, stepped back and allowed Felicia to pass him, then stepped in and closed the door. Everything looked the same. Their suitcases were where they left them. Dane figured that as soon as they packed their toiletries they would be on their way.

He heard Felicia gasp, and spun around. In the far corner of the room sat a dark-haired, dark-skinned man.

"Good morning," the stranger said. "I understand you have been looking for me. My name is Alvarez."

The drapes had been closed and he sat in shadows. All Dane could tell was that he wore dark clothing.

"How long have you been here?" Dane asked.

"It doesn't matter." He looked at Felicia. "You are Adam St. Clair's sister?"

"Yes."

"Adam is very fortunate to have such a loyal family."

"Do you know where he is?" she asked hopefully.

Alvarez slowly shook his head.

Felicia sank down on the side of the bed. Dane walked over and sat in the only other chair in the room.

"Do you know what may have happened to him?"

"He was scheduled to meet a man who was hiding in the mountains. This man had the proof we needed to nail the person who has been controlling the drug route in this area."

"Felipe Santiago," Dane said.

Alvarez straightened in his chair. "You know him?"

"We have just spent the night as his guests at his villa."

"How did you meet him?"

"He found us," Dane replied. "But what about this man Adam was supposed to meet?"

"We can't find him. But we did find Adam's car."

Felicia jumped up. "Where?"

"In the mountains. It had been pushed off the side of one of the mountains. I'm sure whoever sent it over the side hoped it would burn, but there was enough left to identify it."

"Was there any sign of Adam?" Dane asked painfully.

"No."

The three sat in silence for several minutes. Finally Alvarez spoke. "What do you intend to do now?"

"I'm taking Felicia back home."

"I believe that's a good idea. She has no business being here."

"So I've been trying to convince her."

Alvarez stood up. "I'm afraid I can't help you any more than that. At present we are still searching for the man Adam hoped to contact. We don't know if they ever made connections or not. If we can find him, we may still be able to accomplish what Adam set out to do."

The two men looked at each other, silently communicating. Dane stepped forward and held out his hand. "Thank you for coming. I know how dangerous this has been for you."

"Adam would have wanted me to help you. I'm sorry there isn't more." Alvarez stepped behind the drapes and they heard the slight sound of the window being raised. "Good luck," he said in a low voice.

"You, too," Dane responded. He waited for a few moments, then looked out at the patio. Nothing was stirring in the morning light.

"Is this yours?" Felicia asked, and Dane turned around. She was holding an envelope.

"Where did you get that?"

"It was lying here by the phone."

"Maybe one of the maids found it and placed it there."

Felicia opened it with a puzzled expression on her face. A slip of paper and a picture fell out and Felicia leaned over to pick them up.

Her sudden cry seemed to pierce him. He strode to her side just as her legs gave way. She would have fallen if Dane hadn't caught her.

"What is it?" he asked, then realized that Felicia had fainted. Carefully placing her on the bed, Dane leaned over and picked up the contents of the envelope that lay scattered on the floor.

The note contained two words: "Go home." The accompanying picture told its own story. A body lay in a crumpled heap on a mountain road. A car was in the background. Dane recognized the car. He also recognized the body.

It was Adam.

Seven

Warm April sunshine flooded the Texas countryside. Spring showers had turned the grass and trees a vibrant green. Everywhere she looked Felicia saw signs of growth and rebirth.

She pushed the screen door open and stepped out onto the porch, soaking up the view and the scent of springtime. Felicia felt as though she had been through a long, serious illness and was only now beginning to heal.

Her grief for Adam had been an illness of sorts. The pain seemed to have lodged somewhere deep inside her and she wondered if it would ever completely go away.

Sitting down in the porch swing, she gave a slight push that started it swaying gently. Felicia had learned a great deal about life in the past few months.

Had it only been two months since Dane had called her to tell her that Adam was missing? Two months. In that time winter had left and spring had rushed in, turning the brown hills to green, replenishing the earth, nurturing the young, causing a rebirth to take place.

Something similar had begun to happen to Felicia during the past few days—a sense of expectancy and hope for the future. Until then she had been numb to everything that happened around her.

She barely remembered the long trip back home from Monterrey. Felicia had cried until there had been no tears left. By the time of the memorial service she had escaped to the numbness that had protected her from more pain than she could handle, so that she scarcely noticed the number of people who had turned out to pay their respects to Adam.

The official word was that he had been killed in an unfortunate automobile accident, his car going off the road and over the embankment. No one needed to know what he had been hoping to accomplish, why he had been willing to risk his life.

Thanks to men like Alvarez and Lieutenant Delgado, Adam hadn't died in vain. Working together, the authorities had put together the bits and pieces of Adam's last few days. Santiago had been correct—Adam had been double-crossed. The authorities found the man he had gone to meet, and managed to produce enough evidence to have Felipe Santiago arrested without ever revealing Adam's part in the investigation.

Adam would have been pleased.

A gentle breeze caused a few wisps of hair to feather across Felicia's forehead. Being at the ranch had brought Adam closer to her somehow. He was such a part of it. Just as he was a part of her and always would be. Adam would never be dead, not as far as she was concerned. Her memories of him would always keep him alive.

She saw him wherever she looked and she sometimes felt he was just around the corner, or out in the barn, and would be walking into the house at any moment. Felicia could almost feel his presence, he seemed so close, so real. But she knew he was gone.

Felicia sighed. She finally felt able to look ahead now and face the future. No longer could she put off making a decision about her marriage and her career. Her employer had been more than understanding about the delay in her return, but Felicia knew she couldn't keep drifting through the days, waiting for a sign from Dane that he still wanted their marriage.

Dane had reverted to his earlier role of protective older brother. When they had returned to the ranch he had taken her bags to her room without saying a word.

At the time Felicia had been too upset to notice or care. It was only later that she noticed Dane never made any reference regarding their marriage either to her or to Pete or Millie. It was as though the marriage no longer existed.

Perhaps it didn't. Perhaps the United States didn't recognize the legality of their marriage.

Perhaps Dane preferred it that way.

If so, she needed to know so she could plan her next steps. If Dane didn't want her, she knew her job would be her salvation. But if he did, Felicia had considered her options and decided that she would prefer to resign so that she could stay at the ranch. She had always wanted to write and for the past couple of years a storyline had kicked around in the back of her head. If she stayed with Dane, she could try her hand at writing fiction.

If she stayed. What would her life be like? Would he continue to treat her with aloof politeness, as though the hours they had spent in each other's arms had never happened?

If only Dane would tell her what he wanted. He was so seldom home. She wondered if the ranch kept him that busy, or he preferred not to be around her. He was gone by the time she went downstairs each morning and many evenings she was in bed before she heard his truck returning. He rarely came home at noon to eat, although Millie had mentioned to her that he would be home today.

Felicia felt as though she'd lost both Adam and Dane at the same time.

Perhaps today was the day to find out what he expected of her.

Dane sat on a stone outcrop that overlooked the river and the ranch, staring out at the surrounding hills. He'd gotten into the habit of coming up here, trying to come to terms with all that had happened.

Adam was gone. He could no longer hide from that fact. Dane had thought he was prepared for the possibility, but seeing the photograph had shown him differently. A person can never be prepared for something like that, particularly when Dane knew that if he himself hadn't been involved, Adam would never have become a part of the drug problems between the two nations.

Dane also blamed himself for pushing Felicia into a hasty marriage. He hadn't been fair to either one of them. With Adam gone, Dane had to stay on the ranch. Pete was too old to take on the responsibility of running things without Dane's help. However, Dane knew that he had promised Felicia that they would work out something regarding her career and his. But the only solution he could come up with was to let her return to California without him.

He wasn't sure how he'd be able to deal with the separation. The past two months had been bad enough, but at least he saw her every day. Dane had gotten into the habit of going into her room each morning before he left the house, to gain comfort in the knowledge that she was still there.

They had only slept together one night, and yet he found himself waking up repeatedly, reaching for her. He loved her so damned much, but he didn't want to stand in the way of her career. He loved her enough to let her go. He just wasn't sure how well he would survive on phone calls and occasional visits.

Dane glanced at his watch. It was almost noon. Millie would have dinner on the table waiting for him. He shook his head, remembering the strange mood Millie had been in that morning, lecturing him about skipping meals and looking so thin. She'd made him promise to come home for his noon meal.

Seeing Felicia at mealtimes was more painful than going without dinner, although several times he'd driven into town and eaten at The Homestead.

No doubt people were wondering what was happening on the ranch now that Adam was gone. Dane hadn't told anyone about their marriage. He didn't want to embarrass Felicia if she wasn't ready for explanations.

He had noticed that she continued to wear his wedding ring. Did that mean she wanted the marriage to continue? She had made no comment when he placed her luggage back in her room when they returned from Monterrey. They had both been torn up over Adam's death and he thought she might want the added privacy as well as comfort of her familiar room. But as the weeks passed, she'd made no move to resume the marriage relationship. Dane began to wonder if he had pushed her into a relationship she wasn't ready for.

He slowly made his way back to the truck. He could think of many things he'd rather be doing than going home to face Felicia and Millie while trying not to notice Adam's empty chair.

Dane's truck came bouncing up the driveway and came to a stop in front of the house. Felicia's heart began to beat faster at the sight of him. He'd always had that effect on her.

He stepped out of the cab of the truck, slammed the door and with long strides joined her on the porch.

Dane reached up and slowly removed his hat, his gaze never leaving Felicia's face. "Good morning."

The husky quality of his voice made her tremble, reminding her of how he'd sounded when he had whispered to her during their lovemaking.

She raised her eyes to meet his and met his guarded expression. "It's after twelve," she finally murmured. "So it's afternoon."

Dane glanced through the screened door. "I suppose Millie's been counting the minutes so she could scold me for not being here on time."

Felicia stood. "As a matter of fact, she isn't here. Her sister was going into San Antonio today and Millie asked if I'd feed you so she could go with her."

"When was all of this decided?" He held the door open and Felicia walked into the house ahead of him.

"This morning," she replied, glancing back over her shoulder. "Why do you ask?"

"Just wondered." Was Millie trying to force them to spend some time together? He wouldn't put it past her.

Dane stood in the kitchen doorway and watched Felicia as she walked over to the refrigerator and opened it. Reaching inside, she brought out a large pitcher of tea. "Are you ready to eat?" she asked, pulling dishes from the oven and out of the refrigerator to set before him.

Dane nodded and went down the hallway to the bathroom.

When he returned to the kitchen he sat down at the table, looking at all the food. Clearing his throat, he said, trying to lighten the tension between them, "I do believe you've outdone yourself this time, young'un." He picked up a serving dish and began to fill his plate.

"I enjoyed it. Millie seldom needs help in the kitchen. It was nice to have the place to myself."

They ate in silence, each rehearsing what they wanted to say to the other. Felicia cleared their places and served peach cobbler and coffee before sitting down again.

"Felicia?"

"Dane?"

They both spoke at the same time, then stopped.

"Go ahead," he said.

"No, that's okay. What were you going to say?"

They stared at each other in silence for a moment. Then, clearing his throat once again,

Dane said, "I, uh, was just going to ask if you'd talked to your boss lately."

Here it comes, Felicia thought sadly. "No, I haven't, but I need to."

"I suppose you've extended your leave about as long as you can, haven't you?" He toyed with the handle of his cup.

"I suppose so," she murmured.

He took a sip of the coffee, then with deliberation set it down. He looked at her with a calm, unreadable expression. "So what are your plans?"

She stared back at him helplessly, not knowing what to say, not knowing what he wanted her to say. Carefully touching her mouth with her napkin, she finally answered with a question. "What do you want me to do, Dane?"

With a look of frustration, Dane threw down his napkin. "Damn it, Felicia, you're not being fair. I want you to be happy—or at least as happy as you can be. I know your job's important to you—"

"Not as important as you are, Dane. I can always find another job. A husband is a different matter."

He stared at her for a moment in disbelief. "Are you saying you want to stay here—with me?"

"If you want me."

He got up so quickly his chair fell over. He was beside her in two strides, reaching down and hauling her from her chair.

"Of course I want you. I've always wanted you." He lifted her in his arms and started up the stairs.

"You didn't finish your dessert," Felicia managed to say in a slightly shaky voice.

"The peach cobbler can wait. I've got other plans for dessert."

Dane carried her into his room.

She had always loved this room. It had been her mother's. Neither she nor Adam wanted to use it after their mother had died, so it had stood empty until Dane moved in.

Her father had made the bed, her mother had explained to a young Felicia, because he was tired of beds that were too short for him. Dane, too, needed the extra length.

He lowered her onto the bed, then stood there watching her while he unfastened his shirt with self-assured deliberation.

Felicia's heart was pounding so her whole body shook. Dane wasted no time in ridding himself of the rest of his clothing and joining her on the bed. With practiced ease he began to remove her clothing.

"Dane, I think we need to talk."

"Talk," he replied, without pausing in his efforts.

"What I mean is—"

While she hesitated Dane removed her remaining garments.

"Are you sure you want to...I mean...are we even legally married?"

He stopped abruptly and looked down at her. Felicia's hair covered his pillow and he thought of the many nights he'd lain awake imagining her there in bed with him. His gaze met hers.

"Would you rather not be married to me?"

She brushed her hand against his chest, loving the feel of the hard muscles underneath the hair-roughened surface.

"I want very much to be married to you."

"That's good to know," he growled softly, "because you're very much married to me. The marriage was quite legal."

"Then why did you have me sleep in my old room?"

"I didn't *have* you do anything. I left the choice to you. You seemed comfortable enough."

"Oh, Dane. I love you so much." She raised her head a few inches from the pillow and kissed him. "But you don't seem to understand me at all."

He stared down at her for a moment. "You're probably right. All I know is that I love you so damned much I hurt with it." He lowered his head until his lips touched hers. His kiss was warm and possessive.

Felicia relaxed, recognizing that she could teach him to understand her more easily than she could teach him to love her.

His mouth caressed hers, and his tongue traced first her top lip, then her bottom lip, before plunging into her mouth. She shifted restlessly and he caught her thigh between his, clamping it firmly so that she could feel him pushing against her.

He began to kiss her from her nose to her knees—soft kisses, nipping kisses—touching her with an expertise that drove her wild.

Felicia squirmed helplessly as he continued to touch her with his mouth, his teeth, his tongue and his hands, until she thought she would cry out with the marvelous feelings he was causing.

Now he had started a path of kisses that began on the inside of her knee and continued up her inner thigh.

"Oh, Dane, please don't do this to me...Ohh, Dane, I—"

His touch was like setting off a charge of dynamite inside her. Her body quivered, and she cried out with the sensations.

Just when she thought she could no longer stand it, Dane lifted himself higher and buried himself deep inside of her.

Her arms and legs wrapped around him, holding him to her in a convulsive grip. She heard his deep chuckle in her ear and knew that he had done this to her on purpose. Her body was on fire and he was the only one who could put out the flame.

Dane set the pace, never losing control. He played her body like a trained musician plays a beloved instrument, with loving touches and expert delicacy, enjoying the feel of her, the sound of her, the scent and the taste of her.

The fire deep inside her raged out of control, then exploded with a cascade of sparks that caused her body to release all its tension and turmoil. Then the white hot flames turned into cool, soothing tongues of tranquility.

Dane felt her body explode and he could no longer control his reaction to her marvelous response to him. His body took over and he quivered with the force of his excitement as he felt first the heat of the fire, then the soothing coolness of the aftermath of their passion.

They lay there in a tangle of sheets, trying to get their breath, their overheated bodies damp with perspiration.

After a few minutes Dane said quietly, "Are you sure you want to give up your job?"

Felicia lazily turned her head on the pillow and stared at his profile. "I'm sure."

"Won't you be bored staying at home?"

"I don't think so. I intend to try writing a book, something I've wanted to do for years. Besides, I think I'm going to have quite enough to keep me occupied, since we didn't waste any time getting started on our family...."

"What?" Dane jackknifed into a sitting position and stared down at her. "Do you mean...?"

She nodded. "I mean just what you think I mean."

"How do you know this soon?"

"I had my suspicions, so I had some tests run. They called with the results this morning."

"And when did you intend to tell me?" he asked, his gaze direct.

She dropped her eyes. "As soon as I knew where our relationship stood. That sort of news isn't something to just spring on a person."

He shook his head. "Did you really believe our marriage was some sort of trick I played on you?"

"I didn't know what to think. Every since we got back from Mexico you've ignored me."

"Not ignored. I could never ignore you. 'Avoid' is a better word." He touched her hair, running his fingers through it. "We both needed some time. It's been a rough two months."

"I know."

"But my behavior didn't mean I don't love you. I do. Very much." He leaned down and kissed her tenderly on the lips. In a hesitant tone that Felicia had never heard before, he asked, "Are you sorry about the baby?"

She smiled, her face lit as though with a thousand candles. "Good heavens, no. I'm excited about the baby. I just didn't know how to break the news to you. I didn't know what you would think."

He grinned. "I'm delighted about our baby." He leaned over and gave her a long and very possessive kiss.

When he straightened slightly, she laid her palm against his cheek. "I love you."

"I love you, too."

They lay there together, her head on his shoulder, and thought about the coming months.

"Dane?"

"Hmmmm?"

"If it's a boy, could we name him Adam?"

She felt his arm beneath her head tighten. "There was never a question about that."

They were silent for several minutes.

"Wouldn't he have loved being an uncle?"

"Yes."

"If only he could be here to share everything that's happened."

Dane turned so that they were facing each other. "I know, honey. There isn't a day that goes by that I don't miss him, and find myself looking for him."

"I know this is going to sound strange, but I just don't feel he's dead. I mean, I know I saw the picture and everything, but it doesn't seem to make a difference."

"That's just our mind's way of denying what it doesn't want to face, I'm afraid. Eventually we'll come to terms with losing him. It will just take some time."

"You know, if he hadn't disappeared like that I wouldn't have come home."

"Oh, you were bound to come sooner or later."

"No. I was afraid to come home and see you. I couldn't bear to have you treat me with indifference."

"I've never treated you that way."

"I know. But when I left I was convinced you cared nothing for me, and knowing that, I couldn't deal with seeing you, being around you. I needed the miles between us to be able to handle it."

He kissed her again, a lingering kiss that soon scattered all her thoughts. He had the power to push everything else away so that she was conscious only of his presence. She ran her hand across his chest and felt his heart rhythm increase at her touch.

The ringing of the phone was an unwelcome intrusion. She stirred, reluctant to move away from him. He paused long enough to say, "Let it ring. Whoever it is will call back."

"I can't do that. It drives me crazy not to know who's calling." She scooted away from him across the bed and reached for the phone. "H'lo?"

"Felicia? Is that you? What in the world are you doing at the ranch?"

Felicia felt as though she were going to faint. Maybe she had fainted. Maybe this was a dream, one that she would wake up from. The voice on the phone couldn't be—

"*Adam!* Is this Adam?"

Dane sat up with a jerk, staring at her as though she'd lost her senses.

She heard his laugh, Adam's special laugh that no one could possibly duplicate. "You bet it's Adam. What are you doing at the ranch? And where is Dane? I need to talk to him."

"Dane's right here. Where are you?"

"I'm in Del Rio, trying to get home. I seem to be a little short on transportation, plus I'm having a little trouble proving my identity. I don't have any papers on me."

"Oh, God, Adam, you're alive," Felicia said, tears pouring down her cheeks. She handed the phone to Dane, unable to say anything more. She wanted to laugh, and yet tears continued to well from her eyes.

"Adam! Is it really you?" Dane said, taking the phone.

"You'd better believe it's me, although I'm having a heck of a time convincing everyone around here. They keep telling me I'm dead."

"Don't let a little thing like that upset you now. I'm sure everything can be worked out. Where the hell are you?"

"Del Rio. I got as far as the border and was taken into custody, which is a laugh, isn't it? How about coming down here and bailing me out?"

"There's nothing I'd rather do, partner. We'll be there as soon as we can get there."

"What's Felicia doing in Texas? Did she get tired of her job?"

"That's another story. We'll have time to fill each other in once we get you home."

"Sounds good to me, fella. I've been under the weather recently. It'll be good to get back up there and kick back for a few days without doing anything besides eating and sleeping."

Remembering the picture of Adam as he lay slumped alongside his car, Dane was sure 'under the weather' was an understatement.

"See you soon, Adam," he said, and hung up.

Felicia threw herself in his arms. "I can't believe it! Adam is alive. He's coming home. Oh, Dane, he's coming home."

He held her tightly against him, feeling the same elation she was expressing, a thousand questions occurring to him. He patted her bare back and said, "We've got to get going. He's waiting for us to pick him up. Plus I've got to make some phone calls."

While Felicia hurriedly showered and dressed, Dane contacted several people who could help untangle the red tape of getting Adam cleared at the border. Then he showered and dressed, as well.

They were on their way south within the hour.

Dane probably set a new speed record along U.S. Highway 377 and Felicia prayed no one was patrolling the area at that particular time. Dane was in no mood to stop for explanations. Luckily he didn't have to.

By the time they reached the office of the border patrol, Adam's superior had made the necessary arrangements to get him released. He was busy giving his story to two operatives sent over from San Antonio when Dane and Felicia walked in.

Felicia almost cried out when she saw him. There was a scar across his forehead, just below his hairline, that looked red and ugly, but was obviously healing. He looked as though he'd lost several pounds, but he looked wonderful to her.

He stood up when they walked in and she flew into his arms. "Oh, Adam!" Tears cascaded once again.

"You're going to drown me, did you know that?" he asked, a suspiciously husky tone causing his voice to break as he continued to squeeze her.

He reached around her, holding out his hand to Dane, who gripped it with both of his.

"I'm mighty pleased to see you, good buddy," Dane drawled. "You're the only man who would dare hold my wife that way," he added with a grin.

Adam looked down at Felicia, whose smile seemed to add light to an already sunny room. "Your wife? My God. I can't turn my back on you two for a minute, can I?"

"It was more than a minute," Felicia said ferociously. "You remember what Lord Godiva said when his wife arrived home, don't you? 'Your horse arrived hours ago. Where have you been?' "

Adam laughed and the relaxed sound made everyone who heard it smile. "I doubt that my horse made it home, either. No doubt they shot it."

Dane nodded. "Something like that." He glanced around at the other two men, who were watching the reunion with amused smiles, then looked back at Adam. "When are you going to be able to leave?"

Adam glanced over at the men and one of them said, "No reason to stay around here. We were just trying to get some catch-up information. You can phone in a report whenever it's convenient."

Felicia moved to his side and Adam kept his arm clamped around her waist. "Then I'm all for getting out of here myself," he said. She could feel his ribs beneath her hand, as well as the way he was shaking. For all his bravado, Adam was so weak he was barely able to stand.

Trying not to be obvious, she began to move toward the door, coaxing him. "I think that sounds like a great idea. Are you hungry or would you like to head on home?"

Dane opened one of the back doors of the car and Adam gratefully sank down into the well-padded seat. Felicia raised fearful eyes to meet Dane and he shook his head slightly.

After helping her into the front seat, Dane walked around the car. Felicia turned around. Adam's skin was a pasty white. He had closed his eyes and she could see the deep hollows around his eyes and in his cheeks. She watched him for a moment, then softly said, "Why don't you stretch out and take a nap for a while? We can stop to eat a little later if you'd rather."

Adam's eyelids fluttered open and he smiled slightly. "Sounds like a good idea. I just ate a little while ago. Don't seem to have much of an appetite these days."

Felicia was glad the car was large enough as she watched Adam lie down on his side and fall asleep like an exhausted child.

Dane reached over and took her hand, placing it on his thigh. "He's going to be fine, little one. Don't worry. He's tired, but he's on the mend."

"But he's so thin."

"Well, thin's a little easier to cure than dead these days."

"I know. It was just a shock."

"The whole day has been a shock. No sooner do I find out I'm going to be a father, then I discover my baby's uncle is alive and almost well. Too many jolts like that can be hard on a man's system."

Felicia spent most of the ride back home looking over her shoulder at Adam. She couldn't remember when she'd been so happy.

All Adam's strength seemed to have been used up just getting home. Dane helped him into the house, up the stairs and into bed. Millie had returned from San Antonio and could hardly function she was so excited. Pete came in and talked to him a few minutes, and when he left, Felicia could have sworn she saw tears in the old man's eyes.

Millie brought some of her rich homemade soup up for him to eat and Dane and Felicia found they couldn't stay out of his room for long. They just sat there and looked at him, their smiles causing him to grin in return.

"You two look so damned proud of yourselves," he finally said after he'd finished two bowls of soup.

"We're proud of you, Adam," Dane corrected. "We're glad to have you back."

"I'm very glad to be back. There were times when I never expected to see home again."

Dane stood. "Well, we've got a lot of catching up to do, but we don't have to do it all in one day. So why don't we let you get some sleep? Maybe by morning you'll be up to telling us your story."

Adam watched as Felicia slid her arm around Dane's waist. "You two have certainly gotten cosy since I last saw you. This is the longest I've ever seen the two of you in a room together that you weren't fighting."

"I know," Dane agreed. "I discovered I'd rather make love to her than fight with her, though."

"Dane!" Felicia exclaimed, turning red.

Both men laughed.

"In fact, she just informed me earlier today that you are going to be an uncle," Dane went on.

Adam straightened slightly, his smile fading. "An uncle? Wait a minute. How long have you two been married?"

"Long enough," Dane assured him. "We got married the week after you disappeared."

Adam relaxed slightly. "Oh. I'm going to enjoy hearing how you managed that."

Dane laughed. "It wasn't easy. Get some sleep. We'll see you in the morning."

A week went by before Adam felt like doing much more than eating and sleeping. His body demanded recuperation time. Dane kept busy on the ranch and Felicia tried to keep busy, but it was hard. She would find herself tiptoeing upstairs to look in on him, making sure he was all right.

He caught her doing that one day and motioned for her to come in. "I feel like a fool, lying in bed and letting Dane do all the work around here."

"Don't worry about it. As soon as you're on your feet, Dane and I will take off on that honeymoon we never had and let you run things for a while, okay?"

"Sounds good to me. God, it's good to have you back home, Sis."

"That's exactly what I was thinking about you."

"Do you miss your job in L.A.?"

"Not like I thought I would. I've had other things to think about. Besides, I'm with Dane."

"I always thought you put up quite a front where your feelings for Dane were concerned."

"I know. I would probably never have given in to them if you hadn't turned up missing. I flew home to find you."

"You're crazy, you know that? How did you expect to do that?"

"Now you sound just like Dane. No wonder you two get along so well." She grinned at her brother for a moment. "What happened, Adam?"

"It's a long story. One of these days I'll sit down and tell the details to both of you. But the important thing is that I made it to hell and back and lived to tell the story."

"At least you don't have any reason to return. I guess they told you that Santiago was arrested."

"Yes, but he wasn't involved in my disappearance."

"I'm glad to hear that. Despite everything, he treated us well. He could have just as easily disposed of us as turned us loose. I think he was actually concerned about our welfare." Earlier in the week Dane had given Adam a brief summary of their stay in Monterrey.

"Yeah. He's a strange man. I never did understand him." He lay there looking at her in silence for a while. "A baby, huh?"

"Yep."

"That's just like you. Jump in over your head and start a family first thing. You always were headstrong."

"Dane is rapidly taming me, believe me."

"Good for Dane." He grew thoughtful. "You never know why things happen the way they do. I had plenty of time to think about my life, where it was going and what I wanted out of it. I don't suppose a person can go through what I did without coming out of it with a different attitude. I believe you and Dane have discovered what I learned during the past two months. Loving someone and sharing your life with a person can add a powerful dimension to your existence. It gives your life additional depth and meaning.''

"You talk as though you've discovered what love can do."

"I have. I've always known how I felt about the two of you, and knowing you were waiting for me kept me going at times when I was ready to give up. But I need to tell you that I'm going back to Mexico when I'm fully recovered. There's someone there who not only saved my life, but my soul and my sanity. I told her I was coming back for her. I think she doubts that I'll return, but it really doesn't matter if she believed me or not—I'm going."

"She sounds pretty special."

Dane suddenly appeared at the doorway. "Just as I suspected. Here you are entertaining my wife in your bedroom once again. We're going to have to have a talk."

Felicia walked over to the tall man who leaned indolently in the doorway of her brother's room, the same man who had appeared in her life years ago and stolen her heart. Going up on tiptoes, she kissed him, her heart suddenly overflowing with love.

"I don't think you'll ever have to worry, cowboy. I've got my hands full trying to take care of you."

Dane hugged her to him, then looked over her head at her brother, propped up in bed.

The two men exchanged a glance of silent communication. The St. Clair ranch was back in full operation—everyone was home.

* * * * *